Prologue

MICHELLE–PRESENT DAY

MY SUPER SLEUTH INSTINCTS KICKED IN AND I DECIDED TO follow my ex-boyfriend. It was easy, as I had the GPS tracker hidden on his car. It had been there for a couple of weeks. After doubting his sketchy explanations, I finally caved and purchased the dang thing. Putting it to use had been easy. He said his parents lived out in the country. So when I tracked him the first time, I was happy to see he did indeed drive out to the middle of nowhere.

But then, when he drove out there late at night, on a Wednesday, my suspicions rose. My questions were always hedged and never answered to my satisfaction. Who was this man I had spent so much time with? I grew uneasy and that's when I acted.

That's how I found myself sneaking around at night, following him down a gravel road. Surely I was going to get caught. My car was barely moving—a mere five miles per hour—inching along to avoid stirring up dust. The headlights were off and I was only using my parking lights, which wasn't the smartest thing to do. With my luck, I would probably run off the road into a culvert, never to be seen again. Rounding a curve, I came up on a small house. He was parking his car outside, next to another one. I pulled off to the side of the road and parked. I waited a few minutes before braving the next steps.

This was a really bad idea. I should've listened to my gut instincts. Tailing him in the car was one thing, but walking up to that house was another. I pulled out my phone and used the flashlight app to pick my way over to the house so I could spy on him. Peeping into a window—a window of some stranger's home—sunk in like a rock. I was exactly like some creepy criminal, spying on my boyfriend, because I didn't have the courage to ask him the simple question on the phone. "Exactly where are you, Oliver?"

The more I watched, the more intrigued I became. I was glued to the interaction being played out between them. Once I looked, I confirmed it was the right decision to track him. This wasn't his parents' house. The rat was seeing someone. Through the slits in the blinds, I saw him talking animatedly to an attractive blonde. Tall, curvy, and wearing a baseball hat, she was someone I knew! Then they both turned, her back facing me, and he started lifting her shirt. Oh my God, was he undressing her? Suddenly, my blood boiled. My stance shifted and the stupid paint bucket I stood on tipped precariously, forcing me to grab the window ledge. Unfortunately, my head rammed into the damn glass and I lost my grip, falling face first into the huge hedge. Lights blazed on and by the time I pulled myself out of that damn bush, I was staring up at the same two faces I'd been spying on moments before.

"Michelle, what the hell are you doing out here?" Oliver asked, staring down at me.

What in the world was I going to say to that? Brushing

leaves and twigs off me as I stood, I answered, "Maybe I should ask the same of you."

"Jesus. It's not what you think."

"Well then, what exactly does Jesus think?" my smart mouth asked. I stared between my former boyfriend and his very attractive lover and examined their body language. The girl glanced away as soon as our eyes connected. Then she tugged on her ear. Guilty. That's what it was telling me. Oliver stared at me for a second, then grimaced. He was clearly uncomfortable and it was funny, really. I was the one who had been caught creeping around, spying on him. Shouldn't I be the one who felt awkward? No, you big dummy! You weren't caught cheating on your girlfriend! Or ex-girlfriend, as it was.

"Michelle, this isn't . . . I mean we weren't . . ." He blew out a breath.

The other woman said, "You might as well tell her."

"Tell her?" he asked, his voice rising.

"Tell me what? That you've been screwing around on me? That's obvious," I said.

"That's not what we're doing here," he said, gesturing wildly with his hands. He held something in one and a wire flew all around. "Tara and I work together."

"Indeed. We've met. Remember? I'm sure you get a lot of *work* accomplished. At least now I know where you go on all your *family* outings." *Family my ass.* My face burned, but not from embarrassment. I'd scratched the heck out of it when I tumbled into the bushes.

"Michelle, your face. It's bleeding a little."

I dabbed my fingers to it and held them up to the light. Sure enough, blood was present. "Great. Exactly what I need." I was done with him and this conversation. I started to walk away when he grabbed my arm.

"Where are you going? Let me help you clean your face up."

"No, I'm going home." I tugged my arm out of his grasp.

"Honestly, you don't understand. Tara and I were . . . working."

"You expect me to believe that?"

"No! I mean yes."

Shaking my head at him, I said, "You two need to get a better story than that. I'm out of here." I moved past him, but he grabbed my arm again.

"Michelle, I have to explain. Come inside. I can help you clean up your face. Besides, you really don't understand. None of it. Tara and I work together but not in the way you think."

I aimed my finger at him. "See. I knew it. You two are together. Look, you've done enough damage already, Oliver. I thought I was important to you . . . meant something to you. But things never added up. Now I know why. The lies, the secrets. It all makes sense now. You and Tara. Well, for a while I thought we had a chance, but now . . . I'm completely done with you. Let me go."

This time I wrenched my arm from his grasp and didn't give him the chance to stop me. Only his words made me falter. "I love you, Michelle, and it really isn't what you think. Please don't leave."

But I grew a backbone. "Yeah, tell that to your other girlfriend," I mumbled, intending to jog back to my car. Tears clouded my vision. Why did I have to fall for a guy who couldn't be faithful? Why couldn't I fall for someone who only wanted me? And why the hell did I stand on that stupid paint bucket of all things?

Chapter 1

MY BEST FRIEND AND ROOMMATE, SHERIDAN, AND I JUST settled into our new rental home. We were officially Atlanta residents. After spending all those years together getting our degrees, the rewards had paid off. Sheridan landed a great job as a first-grade teacher and I got my dream job working in an advertising firm as an assistant ad copywriter.

"How does this look?" I asked. My arms trembled as I held the heavy print against the wall.

"Perfect," Sheridan said.

We measured where to hang the picture hanger and presto, the print was hung.

Then I gave her a huge squishy hug.

"What was that for?" she asked.

"Just cuz I love you. You're the best roomie I could ask for."

"Well, it goes both ways. You know I love you too. You're my family."

That was true. Sheridan didn't have any family so we'd

unofficially adopted her. She'd faced far more than anyone should at such an early age.

"So, are you ready for your little monsters?" I asked.

"They're not monsters. They're cute little first graders." Then her mouth drooped.

"What?"

"I wish Mom and Dad were here."

"Yeah." I hugged her again. Her parents were both teachers, which was part of the reason she chose the career she was starting tomorrow. "Hey, they're with you every day and they'll be watching over you when you're cracking the whip on those rugrats."

She laughed as I hoped she would.

———

THE NEXT NIGHT, we were sitting around and Sheridan had me falling on the floor in hysterics. Apparently, this quirky little girl in her class named English was funny as hell.

"So I decided we'd play the alphabet game and everybody had to name something that started with each letter. Of course, we started with A. When we got to V, everyone was stumped. Well, everyone but English. She frantically waved her hand yelling, 'I know, I know.' So I called on her and do you know what she said?"

"No clue."

"Vagina."

I died laughing. Sheridan had to keep a straight face but it was difficult, to say the least.

"Oh, my God. I can't even imagine."

"It got worse."

"How?"

"All the kids started talking about penises and vaginas then. I was mortified."

"Sounds like first grade porn."

"Shut up. It was horrific."

"No wonder you're guzzling all the wine tonight."

With that, she downed the rest of her glass. But the expression on her face indicated that she was loving her role as a teacher.

"What about your day?" she asked.

I couldn't keep the grin off my face. "Well . . . my boss keeps telling me my brain was made for advertising."

"That's fantastic, Michelle."

"Yeah, and I love it. I love the creative process, you know? Coming up with how to decide which demographics we're going to target and then working up the copy for it. It's fun."

"Did you ever think we'd be here, doing the things we both love?"

"Yeah, I did." I knew some day, if we both worked hard enough, which we did, we'd end up with jobs we wanted. But I especially wanted Sheridan to get her dream job because her real life had been shattered too many times to count.

Chapter 2

MICHELLE

IT TOOK ME FOREVER TO PERSUADE SHERIDAN TO GO OUT with me. It was a Friday night and we were hanging in my favorite club. The music blared and we celebrated the weekend. Cosmos flowed and we danced a bit. Sheridan noticed the father of one of her students in here. I was shocked to find out he was our age and wasn't an older dude, not to mention he was hot as hell.

"He's the jerk I told you about. The dad of cute little English. The one at the parent-teacher conference."

"Oh, right." Apparently, he treated her like crap, even after showing up late for the meeting. He was a total assface. "Boy is he checking you out."

"I doubt that."

"Uh, yeah he is." And he totally was.

Not much later, a sexy hipster with dark hair and dreamy blue eyes who I'd met in here before made his way over to us. He'd been with a group of people the last time though and things never worked out where we could actually chat.

I lusted after him that night and was disappointed it didn't work out. Tonight he wore low cut jeans that hugged his hips along with a black T-shirt that showed off his hot body, but what I loved best about him were his dark-framed glasses. For some reason I'd always been attracted to men who wore specs.

"Hi, my name's Oliver Griffith."

"I'm Michelle McDaniels. We've met in here before."

"Yeah, but I didn't think you remembered."

How could I forget someone like him? Just looking at him made my stomach quiver.

"Of course I remember."

We got reacquainted with each other, talking about our respective jobs. He worked in IT and fit the part, a total sexy geek, enough to make me clench my thighs together. I was completely intrigued by him and wanted to know everything I could. He was sweet, smart, and those damn glasses had me wanting to rip them off and kiss him. His messy dark hair, the way it fell over his brow, had my fingers itching to push it back in place, and a few times he had to ask me the same question twice because I was caught staring at him.

"Would you like to dance?"

"I'd love to," I answered, very ladylike, when I wanted to say *fuck yeah*.

Before long, we were wrapped in each other's arms on the dance floor, kissing. I couldn't keep my hands off him. He was lean and hard, not bulky like some guys, and my fingers twitched to steal a feel of his skin. I didn't want to scare the poor guy off, but God help me he was the best thing since Cosmos were invented. The man could kiss— the toe curling, sex tingling, heart-throbbing kind. Drinks kept flowing and not much later, I caught Sheridan's eye to let her know that Oliver and I were going to Uber it out of there. I wanted to touch every part of him and be indecent about it too.

———

Oliver

WHEN I WALKED into the club and saw her, I knew she'd be mine. It wasn't supposed to happen like this. I wasn't supposed to get involved, so they said. The last time I met her here I did my best to avoid her. She was the most gorgeous woman I'd ever seen. But fate wasn't on my side. Tonight, there she stood, exactly like she was waiting for me.

Her long black hair gleamed under the lights of the dance floor and I wanted to run out there like an idiot, claiming her as mine. Watching her lithe body move to the rhythm of the music was more than any man should have to bear, and I almost . . . almost turned and went home. But I didn't. I was either making the greatest mistake of my life or it would be the best thing I ever did.

When I introduced myself, I wondered if she'd remember. She did. The exotic scent of flowers wafted around me and I realized I needed to pull my shit together or else I would look worse than the ridiculous geek I already was. I wanted to impress her, not push her away. But she was sweet and acted like she wanted to be with me. Her gray eyes sparkled when she spoke, and her plump pink lips were almost too much to see. If only I could have just a taste, I told myself. But I was a fucking liar. I knew one taste would never be enough.

"Would you like to dance?" What I really wanted to ask her was, *would you like to fuck*? But I knew where that would lead. I'd end up with her high heel jammed up my ass.

She was with her roommate and glanced over to her a time or two. I hated selfish, inconsiderate people, but for once in my life, I wanted this girl to be that way tonight. I wanted Michelle to only care about me.

"I'd love to," she said. Her eyes shimmered as I reached for her hand.

When we hit the dance floor, all bets were off. I was right about her mouth. Her fucking mouth was more than I'd imagined. She tasted sweet—like the Cosmos she'd been drinking—and I wanted all of her. My restraints flew out the window and my lips and tongue were on and in her as though they were meant to be there. Her hands pulled me close and I knew . . . I knew she belonged to me.

Michelle

WE HOPPED in the Uber and headed straight on over to his place. He shared a house with his roommate not too far from where I lived in the Brookhaven area of Atlanta.

Our hands were joined the entire way there. I could scarcely take in air, being this close to him. All I could think of were how his kisses made me feel and how I melted into his arms when we danced. I never wanted that feeling to end. Here we were, headed to his house, and my heart pounded in anticipation. Maybe it was the alcohol leading me down this road to lust, but damn did I want this man. There was something about him that was different. He looked at me as though I was the only person on Earth.

The car stopped in front of a cute little bungalow and

we got out. Even in my semi-inebriated state, it didn't slip past me that he was every bit the gentleman. Maybe it was because he wanted to get in my pants, and in all likelihood would, but I paid attention to those kinds of things.

When we got inside, I noticed the details. His home was orderly and well organized. Things were put together nicely. There weren't any clothes lying around. No beer cans sat on the coffee table, or leftover pizza boxes with day-old pizza in them. Everything was so . . . clean. I was impressed.

"Can I get you something? A glass of wine? A drink?" he asked.

I wanted to say *you*, but instead, I answered, "How about a water?" I'd already had plenty of alcohol as it was. Best to play it safe.

"Sure thing."

I followed him into the kitchen and found it to be very clean too. No dirty dishes in the sink, or old food left out. I was starting to like him even more. He fixed us both glasses of ice water and we stood there gazing at each other. Then suddenly I found myself in his arms as he kissed me.

I grabbed his shirt and pulled it up to slide my hands underneath. My fingers found smooth skin wrapped over taut muscles. I was dying to see what he looked like without his shirt. Only I didn't want to appear overly aggressive. His hot skin called out to me and my tongue wanted to taste him. What the heck was wrong with me? I'd never had such a potent reaction to a man before. It must be the alcohol. I needed to remember to stay away from those Cosmos.

"You're the first person I saw tonight when I walked into the club," he said. "Couldn't tear my eyes off you."

"Really?"

"You were dancing and you're more beautiful than

anyone I've ever seen." He ran his hand down my hair and then brushed it off my face. "I've never seen hair like yours on anyone before. It's like satin. And your eyes. They sparkle, you know? Come to life when you speak."

I couldn't respond as I stared at his sexy-as-hell mouth. Behind full lips a glimpse of his perfect teeth could be seen. Then he smiled and I nearly died. High cheekbones created amazing shadows beneath, and he had one tiny dimple on his right cheek. My mouth automatically responded in a smile. A long fringe of hair fell forward over his forehead and I pushed my fingers through it, finding it to be soft and thick.

"I have to say I love your glasses." My throat was thick with desire.

"You do?" he asked, his tongue poking the inside of his cheek.

"Yeah. I think they're super sexy."

"Sexy, huh?"

"They impart a certain intelligence and I'm attracted to smart guys. You did say you were in IT, right?"

"I did."

"See, you guys are usually nerdy."

He ran his tongue over his lips, then said, "I'm a huge nerd." His dilated pupils began to narrow slightly as I stared at them.

"No, not nerdy at all. You're hot. Extremely hot."

"Have you looked at me?"

"I'm staring at you." Our mouths were only an inch apart and all I wanted was to taste his lips. "Kiss me, Oliver."

"Michelle, I want more than your kisses."

"Then why don't you go for it?" The words came out in a whisper.

He took a step back. "This is new. And I want this to be right between us. You know?"

"Yeah, so do I. But I have a feeling it will be."

And I did. I couldn't answer why. I just . . . did. Before we moved to his bedroom, he asked me a couple of things. "Are you sure you won't have any regrets?" And, "Will you hate me in the morning?"

My response to him was, "I won't hate you if you don't run away, and no regrets because I want more than your kisses too."

"There won't be any running, I can promise you that," he said.

And boy was I right about my feelings. Only I had Oliver pegged wrong. He may be a nerd in life, but he certainly wasn't in the bedroom. We did it on the floor. The bed. Against the wall. Oliver was a beast.

"Michelle, close your eyes and do not open them. Bend over the bed and hold on for your life." This was after I sat on his face, and he'd already fucked me like a rodeo champ.

I didn't even think to refuse him, because by this time I'd figured out that Oliver not only was smart, he was an expert at knowing how to please me. He jacked up my hips to meet his own and plunged into me, hard. My pussy ached for him already. His voice struck a chord in me. Just the way he spoke had me ready for him again. And that was just plain and simple crazy as hell. I was raw and swollen, but needy too. When he pushed in deep, he hit all my buttons hard, and soft. I panted, my eyes squeezed tightly shut. My toes barely hit the floor as he held me up high, pulling me into his thrusts. Each time he did it, my throbbing nipples scraped the sheets, making them beg for more. I wanted to pinch and tug them, only I couldn't because I needed my hands to hold myself on the bed. My teeth ground together as I strived to reach my climax. I was close . . . so damn close.

Then he plunged all the way in and pressed against me, staying deep inside me. My clit thrummed, needing attention.

"Please," I begged. "I need to come."

He chuckled. "Yeah, like you haven't done that yet."

"No, I need more. Now."

He pulled out and slammed in hard. "Like this?"

"More."

He reached around me and dipped low to reach my clit. Then he slid into me again as he put pressure on my little bud. "Yes. There. More."

He rubbed it and pumped into me at a steady pace. But the finger he popped in my back door really was a pleasant surprise. I lowered my chest so my nipples dragged across the bed. And that was exactly what I needed. It set me off while those inner muscles squeezed him, as he got his own. He finally set my feet down and I crawled onto the bed as he went to the bathroom. I imagined he was removing the condom he put on earlier. Then he was back, pulling me into bed properly and curling behind me when he started to pinch and tug on my nipples.

"God, I was dying for that when you were inside me."

"Sorry, I don't have enough arms."

"Yeah, I needed an octopus."

"Maybe we should try some nipple clamps for fun."

"Maybe so. I've never tried them."

"I haven't either. But from what I've read, they bring pleasure when you remove them. Tomorrow." He nuzzled my neck and kissed it. "You're so fucking sexy. I'd like to try all sorts of things with you."

"I was thinking the same of you. That you're sexy. And

I'm willing to try different things too, as long as it's not too far out."

"Hey, Michelle, no regrets, right?"

"None."

"You're not going to dart out of here when the sun rises, are you?" he asked, his warm breath fanning my neck.

Not a chance in hell of that.

"I wasn't planning on it. Why?"

"Because I want to date you. See you again. A lot of agains. That's why."

I rolled over to look at him. "I like that idea." Then I kissed him and snuggled in for some sleep.

The sun came up and we were wrapped together like a taco within a burrito. It was the first time I'd slept with someone like that and didn't feel weird waking up. Did that mean something, or was I over thinking things? Time would tell, I supposed.

Chapter 3

MICHELLE

Oliver and I quickly became almost inseparable. We spent just about every night together and when he asked us to be exclusive, I readily agreed.

"You're good with it? It's not too soon?"

Smiling, I said, "No, I'm very good."

He relaxed at my words. "Good, because the thought of you with another man doesn't go over too well with me. And besides, I can't seem to get enough of you."

That made me super happy. I didn't want him hopping in bed with anyone else, either. Sheridan had our house to herself most of the time. Hopefully, she was enjoying the peace and quiet.

Oliver and I did almost everything together and shared a lot of intimate details about each other. I even told him that I'd never been in love before.

"Never?"

"Never. I've dated a lot, but no one ever affected me enough to say the words. It was never there. What about you?"

He laughed. "Once. When I was ten. I was in love with

Deanna Johnson. She sat in front of me in the fourth grade. I used to play with her black curls. Until her mom sent a note to school asking the teacher to get me to stop. My desk was moved to a different row. That ended our relationship."

I threw my head back and laughed. "What—did you just play with her hair all day?"

"Well, sort of. It was right there where I could touch it and she was perfect. I thought she liked it. Apparently she didn't." He made a goofy face and I laughed again.

"You were a nerd."

"Oh, yeah. My mom had to give me the talk about when to touch girls and when not to touch them. After that, I noticed how the girls laughed at me. That's when I figured out I was really a geek."

"Aw. Well I think you're perfect."

About a month later, he told me he had to go to some family thing. I figured waiting he'd invite me, but I was wrong. I was more than a little disappointed since we spent so much time together, were so close, and I'd met all the people he hung out with. I just assumed meeting his family would be next. If mine lived near town, he would've met them already. It hurt my feelings, but if he noticed, he didn't mention it. So I went back to the house I shared with Sheridan.

"No Oliver today?" she asked.

"He's visiting his parents. They live an hour away. Do you think it's weird he didn't invite me?"

She didn't answer.

"You can be honest. My feelings are hurt. You know if Mom and Dad lived that close, I would've taken him there for Sunday dinner already."

"True. It is sort of odd, but maybe his parents are strange."

"I hadn't thought of that."

"I wouldn't worry about it. Guys are different than women when it comes to this stuff."

She was probably right.

Oliver called later and I acted as if nothing were wrong.

"How was your family?"

"Oh, they're great. I miss you. Wanna come over?"

"Ordinarily, I would say yes. But I'm going to spend some time with Sheridan. Tomorrow though, okay?"

Sheridan and I ended up going to the movies and ran into that sexy dad. He was there with his daughter. And was he ever fine, in a completely different way than Oliver, and he stared at Sheridan for days. I thought he had more than a passing interest in his kid's teacher, but I kept my mouth shut. She'd never believe me anyway.

When I told her how hot he was, she told me he was pretty much an ass, but the kid was over the top all kinds of cute rolled up in sweet.

"I could just eat her alive. She is the greatest thing ever and it's so hard not to play favorites in class," she said.

Later that night, he texted Sheridan and offered to help her get her car fixed. Her car was about ten years old and she'd been having issues with it. Apparently he knew someone who could help.

"Seems to me, Mr. Ass is turning into Mr. Nice and has some interest in you."

"He doesn't. He just wants to look good for his kid."

"Yeah. Go on and fool yourself, but you can't fool me, Sheridan Monroe."

"Just because you have a sexy computer geek for a boyfriend who is nice to you doesn't mean every guy is like that."

"Did I say anything about that? And that reminds me.

Oliver and his roommate are throwing a Halloween party and I keep forgetting to invite you."

She pointed to her crutches and boot. Sheridan broke her foot a while back and had to use those things for a while. "Uh, I appreciate the offer, but I'll only go if I'm done with those. Being at a party on crutches would not be my idea of having fun."

"Okay, but if your doctor gives you the go ahead, you'll come then?"

She shrugged. I felt terrible for her because she'd been so down in the dumps lately. The broken foot really threw her. Then she had car trouble. Her financial situation was awful to begin with. She didn't need any added bills. I kept hoping things would turn around for my girl.

The following weekend was Halloween and Oliver's party was that night. I was almost ready in my Raggedy Ann costume and asked Sheridan for a once over.

"What's Oliver dressing as?"

"Raggedy Andy," I said.

"Oh, no he isn't."

"It was his idea." I almost died when he suggested it, but he was so stupid cute I didn't know what to say. Then he pulled out the nipple clamps and told me if I didn't say yes, I would be in big trouble. But I was in big trouble anyway. He stripped off my shirt and bra, put the clamps on, and fucked me as only a computer nerd could. Byte by byte. And I mean with teeth. My ass was all marked up. Still was. He said he had another surprise for me tonight. I couldn't even imagine. Turned me into a huge nipple clamp fan, too.

When I got to his house, he opened the door and I cracked up. His version of Raggedy Andy was different than mine. His clothes were hot, torn, and ragged. He did wear a yarn wig and put dots on his face, but that's where it ended. Everything else was totally manly. There I stood in my ridiculous little ruffled dress, red and white stockings, and red yarn wig.

"Nice, McDaniels. Very nice. Come with me."

"Am I the first one here?"

"Well, yeah. No one else will be here for another hour or more."

"Oh."

He took my hand and we went up to his room.

"I have a surprise for you."

"Hmm, is Andy gonna get Ann a little dirty?"

"Damn right he is."

He disappeared for a minute and came back with something in his hand. Then he held it out and I stared at it.

"What's that?" It was a little purple thing with a jewel on one end and an odd shape at the other.

"An itty bitty butt plug. Just for you."

"That's a butt plug? It's so fancy. And little. You're going to plug my butt?"

He chuckled. "That and other things."

"I'd always thought those things were a lot bigger than that."

"They come in all different sizes."

"My, you're a wealth of knowledge."

"Michelle, my scrumptious little gumdrop, there is a wealth of information on this thing known as the World Wide Web." Then he nibbled my neck, which, of course, led to a heated kiss.

"So, what are you going to do with that butt plug?" I asked.

"Mmm. I thought I'd stick it in your ear." His face, with all the black freckles he'd painted on, was so comical I broke out in a loud snort.

"My ear, huh. Won't I look sort of silly?"

"Yeah, especially when people ask you why you have a butt plug sticking out of there." Then my strong boyfriend lifted me up and I wrapped my red and white striped legs around his waist. "Gumdrop, I thought I might put it in your ass and you could wear it to the party."

Gumdrop?

I nearly choked. "What? You are joking, right?"

"Actually, I'm not. Your ass filled with that tiny thing gives me a fucking boner just thinking about it."

"Oliver, there is no way in fucking hell I will wear it to the party. How will I sit?"

A devilish glint was in his eyes. "I was thinking you'd be standing most of the night."

He was crazy. "You're whacked."

"Yeah, I am. Over you."

"That's great. But you can be crazy about me without me wearing a butt plug at the party. Holy crap, Oliver."

He only laughed at me. "It would be so much fun to watch you squirm with every step."

"I have a better idea. Why don't you wear it?"

"That's not a good idea at all."

"Why not?" I asked.

"Because it would take the fun out of me being able to watch *you*. That was the whole idea behind it. The thing is, when you're aroused, it's like . . . well honestly, it's inde-scribable."

"I don't want to be aroused all night. That would be torture."

"How about we put it in later on?"

"Oliver, you've lost your mind."

"I've already admitted that. I'm crazy for you, babe. What can I say?"

I scratched my head under the hot yarn wig. Ugh. Was

he saying he's like really crazy for me as in love with me? He hadn't said those exact words so I didn't know. And I wouldn't ever second-guess that.

"I'm making no promises as far as wearing a butt plug. Playing with it is one thing. But wearing it . . . whole other ball game there." And I was firm on that.

"Okay. I'll find some other way to get you all hot and bothered, my dirty little Ann." Then he kissed me again.

Honestly, I just wanted to tell him to stand there and look innocent wearing his sexy glasses. That was enough to soak my panties in a heartbeat.

We headed back downstairs and not much later the guests trickled in. Zack's date came and she was dressed as a White Walker from *Game of Thrones*. Her make-up was amazing. I could never be that creative. Zack was dressed as Jon Snow, so that worked well. There were tons of zombies, which was no surprise, a few vampires, cheerleaders, football players, a SWAT team member, a hazmat guy, and too many others to name.

Most of the people who were invited were friends of Zack and Oliver's either through work or their neighbors. Their neighborhood, much like the one I lived in, was filled with young professionals, just out of college or not too many years past that, and Oliver and Zack seemed to have blended right in. I mingled with as many people as I could, eager to meet and chat with them. The truth was I'd never had a problem meeting guys. Keeping them was another issue. Yeah, I'm spoiled and probably slightly selfish. So this time around, because I really liked Oliver, I was putting in that extra effort. And because of that, it was the first time I noticed it—the fact he may have been hiding something from me.

"So why didn't you invite any of your family?" I asked.

"Huh?" He stared at me blankly.

"Your brother or sister? You told me y'all were close. I would've thought they'd be here."

He rocked back on his heels and slowly nodded. "Oh, that. They both had other parties to go to. Hey, let's go out back. There's a fire in the pit and I need another beverage." He took my hand and pulled me along behind him. No question about it, he'd changed the topic on me. But why? There was definitely some issue with his family he didn't want me to know. Tonight wasn't the time to talk about it, so I let it slide.

When we got outside, a group of people were hanging out by the fire. They were talking up a storm, but when we got there, the talk quieted down.

"I know you all are yapping about computer junk. Go on, don't let me stop you," I said.

One of them, a blonde, says, "No, I'm glad for the interruption. We talk this stuff all day. I'm sick of it."

"Then I'm glad I could be of help." I held up my cup and we did a fake toast.

"I'm Tara. I work with Oliver."

"Nice to meet you. You must be a fan of *The Walking Dead*." She was dressed as a zombie, so it was hard to see what she looked like.

"Who isn't?" she asked.

I raised my hand up and wiggled my fingers.

"No way. How can you not be?"

I explained why I didn't like the show and how it had to do with all the plot holes. "I think it would've been so easy for them to fix it and since they didn't, I had to give it up. If you've ever lived at ground zero during and after a hurricane, and then go without power or water for a week, you understand that some of the things they did weren't possible."

She studied me for a moment, then nodded. "I guess

you do have a good reason for it. But I'm so invested now I'll keep going until the end."

"Oh, you should. It's with any show. Once you love it, you're hooked."

Oliver moved in between us and said, "Hey, enough about you two. Let's talk about me."

"Oh, brother," Tara said. Then she wandered off and talked to another zombie.

"You wanna go inside and dance?" Oliver asked.

"Why not?"

The music was playing and they pushed back all the furniture to make room for dancing in the living room. A slow song came on, so Raggedy Ann and Raggedy Andy took the floor. We swayed and twirled and I adored every minute in his arms. He pulled out his phone and we took a ton of selfies too.

Later that night, after everyone was gone and it was just the two of us, alone in his room, he told me I was the sexiest one at the party.

"Oh, I don't know. I saw a few hot zombies, one very hot Daenerys Targaryen, and even a sexy Princess Leia including the giant honey buns in her hair."

"Yeah, but they didn't compare to my yarn-haired beauty."

He said it so sincerely I found myself believing him and falling for him even more. I touched his face and kissed him.

The top of my dress was elasticized so all he had to do was pull it down and slide the thing off. That left me in my bra and those ridiculous red and white striped tights. A giggle leaked out of me and I asked, "Now do you think I'm sexy?"

"Totally. I love these, Gumdrop."

"Hey, where did this Gumdrop come from?"

"That red wig reminded me of candy."

"Hmm. I would've thought you'd come up with something more romantic."

"How about this? Put that sexy mouth of yours back on mine. I want to kiss you while I pull these little things off you."

That's exactly what he did and I took care of his pants too. Good thing he went commando, my nerdy guy.

"I didn't know geeks went commando," I said.

"I didn't either." He started to kiss me again, but I put my hand on his chest and stopped him.

"Oliver. Can I just say you were the sexiest guy at the party? By far." I ran a finger over his bottom lip and rolled it down a little. "I think you're . . . I'm very attracted to you."

His mouth crash landed on mine and stole away my breath. I was so surprised I barely noticed that he backed me against the wall. His expert fingers found my sex and discovered I was already wet for him.

"I love your silkiness. So wet. I can't wait to take you and make you mine." His voice sent a ripple of shivers down my spine as he slowly slid a long finger inside me. "I could touch you for days and not get tired of it."

My breathing ramped up, and so did his movements. He pulled me over to the side of the bed and knelt between my legs. His finger was soon replaced by his mouth, where he tongued my pussy and I watched in fascination. Large sky-blue eyes looked into my own as he continued to suck on my clit and finger me, while his thumbs spread me wide for him. And I could not pull my eyes away. It was so delicious seeing him do these things to me. My blood raced, my heart pounded, and I wanted as much of this as he was willing to give. My fingers pinched and tweaked my nipples to soothe their ache. And all too soon, my climax roared into me, those familiar spasms overtaking me as I called out his name.

"Don't move. I want you just as you are."

He stood and took his heavy cock in hand for a few seconds as he stared at me, then he wrapped himself in a condom, and drove all the way inside of me as I sat on the edge of the bed. But it wasn't enough. I fell back and he grabbed my ankles, placing them both on one shoulder. The friction was tight and amazing.

"Ahh," he groaned. His hips rocked into me, and suddenly I had the urge to try that butt plug. So I suggested it. His only response was, "Later." Soon, I was lost in the rhythm he produced, the fullness of him inside of me, the sensation of it all. He pressed on my clit again as he pumped into me, hard and strong, and I met each of his thrusts gladly. My nipples were rocks, screaming for attention. So I complied by pinching them, but one of his hands brushed one of mine away and took over. It eased the ache and soon my muscles were clamping down on him in an epic climax. He ground his cock to the hilt into me and when he moaned deep in his throat, I knew he was getting off too. I felt him throbbing inside me, as my muscles spasmed around him. When it passed, he pulled out and went to the bathroom.

I curled on my side, exhausted and sleepy. He picked me up and pulled the covers over us.

"Time for bed, sleepy head," he said.

"Yeah. Can't keep my eyes open."

The last thing I remembered was him kissing my neck softly and telling me how gorgeous I was. Not a bad way to drift asleep.

Chapter 4

MICHELLE

Sheridan and I sat in the living room and I listened to her tell me what was going on in her life. When she told me about Beck's—her single daddy—proposition, I didn't want to show my shock. They'd gone out a few times after he kept doing nice things for her, but this . . . this was way beyond what I'd imagined.

"You're going to do it. You love that kid so much, there's no way you'll refuse him," I said.

"I don't know if I can. English is adorable, but what he's proposing is a pretty huge leap. Beck's custody battle is his own to fight. I shouldn't feel like I have to take it on."

"No, you shouldn't. But I know you and I understand how you sometimes look at things. You're probably thinking about English right now and worrying whether or not her father will lose custody of her. Besides, look at him. He's gorgeous."

"That shouldn't matter. Besides, it's crazy!" She practically screamed it at me.

Shrugging, I said, "So? He has good reasons."

"You honestly think I should do it?"

Holding out my hand, I said, "Whoa. Hang on a minute. That is not what I said. What I did say was you're going to do it because you adore that little girl. I don't believe you would let anything jeopardize her relationship with her dad. End of story."

Sheridan stared at me like I was the crazy one. She wrung her hands. "I don't know what to do."

"Do you have to decide right this minute?"

"No, but if I don't, I'll have a stomach ache for days."

She'd always been anxiety prone, ever since her mother died.

"Okay, then why don't you do a pros and cons list?"

"I did. Look." She handed me a sheet of paper and I checked it out.

"Damn, girl, there are only two cons on here and the rest are pros. So sexy single dad Beck isn't so bad after all, is he?"

She stuck her bottom lip out and nodded.

"Don't pout. What about the kid? English?"

"Yeah. She's precious. So cute. I hate to play favorites but it's hard not to."

"You are so done. And I'm not saying another word."

She cringed as a stress line formed on her brow. "You think I'm doing the right thing?"

"Only you can answer that. Sometimes you just gotta go with your heart. Ya know?"

"Uh huh. Crazy as this sounds, I'd do anything for English. And that's where Beck and I have common ground."

"Better pick up your phone and call him before you chicken out."

She chewed on her lip for a second or two and then did it. I was pretty shocked to say the least, but I didn't let on. After I gave it some thought, Sheridan was so kind and generous, it didn't really surprise me too much. He picked her up so they could discuss things, setting the wheels in motion.

On the day they were leaving for their "trip" as she was calling it, Beck came to pick her up. As he was carrying her bags to the car, I asked to have a word in private with him. Sheridan looked at me oddly, but I waved her off and told her he'd be right out. When she was gone, I was quick with my words.

"Beck, she's been through a lot. Not your ordinary stuff that young people our age deal with, but I'm talking real bad stuff. Heartbreaking, soul-cracking situations. I'm not sure how much she's shared, it's not my place to tell you, and I won't. But what I will tell you is this. I understand why you two are doing what you're doing and I respect that. What I won't respect is if you so much as hurt one single hair on her head. I will come after you with everything I have. I'm talking I will literally crush you. Do I make myself clear? Treat her like a queen or you will regret ever being born."

The man, who looked like Adonis, only stared and nodded. You would've thought I gut punched him. Maybe I did. Or maybe no one ever spoke to him that way. Whatever the case, I didn't care. My only concern was that my bestie didn't get her heart ripped out.

Later that day, I spoke with Oliver, wondering if he was going to invite me to his parents' sometime over the Thanksgiving weekend to meet them. We were together constantly, spending almost every night together, and he'd talked about how much he wanted to meet my family. I'd told him he's more than welcome, but he changed the subject every time. It was getting to be a little more than annoying and I was beginning to wonder if he was hiding some kind of an issue. He never mentioned meeting his family. Since I was leaving that evening to go see my own mom and dad, I was hoping he'd bring it up.

"Well, have a Happy Thanksgiving."

"You too, Gumdrop. Don't eat too much turkey."

"I won't."

That was it.

———

Oliver

THE TOPIC of Thanksgiving was more than awkward, not being able to invite Michelle to my parents'. I knew she was fishing for an invitation, but I avoided it altogether. There was nothing more I wanted than to spend those days with her, and being away from her was going to kill, but I didn't have a choice. The worst part of it was I knew it hurt her. I hoped to mend those areas, and maybe soon. She meant more to me than anyone I'd ever been with. I kept hoping she wouldn't run from me and would trust me long enough to get through the next few months.

———

Michelle

THE TWO-HOUR DRIVE TO MY PARENTS' was spent obsessing over him. What was the deal? Was he ashamed of me?

By the time I pulled into the driveway, Mom was waiting at the front door, all smiles, and excited to see me. I, on the other hand, was depressed and sullen.

"What's wrong, sweetie?"

Mom knew me well. I'd had phone conversations about him and she passed it off as a man thing.

"I wouldn't worry about it. He's probably not thinking too much along those lines. Boys are like that, you know. Your father never once thought to bring me to meet his parents until my dad asked to meet his. Then he wanted to know why."

That was somewhat encouraging news.

"You really think so?"

"Oh, yes. Christmas will be the clincher. I'm sure he'll invite you over then. Some people just think of Thanksgiving as another meal."

"Speaking of, what are our plans?"

We discussed the day's adventures, as I called them, because they entailed going over to Dad's brother's house. My aunt and uncle had five kids and they were all hellions. I was waiting for the call from Mom telling me they had burned the house down. Both my aunt and uncle thought the kids were angels. They were more like demons on wheels.

"Is Grandma going?"

"Nope. She is going to the buffet at Serenity Village." It's the retirement community she moved into after Grampy died.

"She wants to do that?" I asked, shocked.

"Why yes. She has a sweetheart there." Mom waggled her brows. "He is playing his accordion during dinner for everyone, so she doesn't want to leave. Then later in the evening they are having a Sexy Bingo tournament. She's determined to win money."

"Grandma has a sweetheart?"

"I didn't tell you?"

"No!"

Mom filled me in on Grandma's love life. His name was Harold and he was quite the charmer. He was an expert polka dancer, an accordion player, and he made wiener dogs out of balloons. All the women were after him because he was one of the few men there who had his own teeth and could still hear.

"Your grandmother swore she heard a rumor that he had an unlimited supply of Viagra too."

"Oh my God, Mom. That was way too much information."

"Oh, come on, Michelle. I think it's kind of cute."

"Eww, no."

"Honey, just because she's old—"

I covered my ears and yelled, "Staaaahp! I mean it."

Mom only laughed. Dad must've heard, because he came into the kitchen asking what the ruckus was about. When Mom explained, he chuckled.

"Yeah, she's a spry one, isn't she, that grandma of yours?"

"I can't do this. I'm going to put this in my room."

I grabbed my bag and headed for my old room, the one that still had my pink comforter and lacy curtains because that's what I wanted when I was sixteen. It made me wonder when Mom was going to redecorate in here.

When I reemerged thirty minutes later, Mom was putting a couple of pumpkin pies in the oven.

"Is there anything I can help with?" I asked.

"Are you hungry?"

"Starved."

"Barbecue from the Three Little Piggies?"

That was our usual the night before Thanksgiving dinner.

"Yass!"

Dad called it in and went to pick it up while I sat at the

counter and drank a beer. Mom did some last-minute things that she swore she didn't need help with. I drooled as I watched her assemble a sweet potato casserole while the aroma of pumpkin pies baking wafted through the room.

"Oh my God, I don't think I can wait until tomorrow to eat that stuff."

"You don't have to," Mom said with a sly look. "I made extra." She pulled one out of the fridge.

"You're a dog. I don't need all those extra calories."

"Pfft. Look at your skinny self. You're exactly like Grandma. You'll never have a weight problem. So tell me about Oliver."

She knew most of it because I talked to her every day just about. When I pulled out my phone and showed her some pictures, though, she fanned herself.

"Phew, he sure is a cutie."

"Right? Look at his eyes. I'm not sure if you can even get the full effect behind his sexy glasses, but they're a beautiful shade of blue. Oh, Mom, he's so pretty."

She smacked me on the hand. "Don't you call that man pretty. I raised you better than that. He's handsome. Yummy. Downright sexy or a hunk. That's what we called them in my day. But pretty he is not. He's too manly to be called pretty."

"I know what you're saying, but he is pretty. His face is perfect."

"Perfect is fine too, but do not ever call a man pretty. You hear?"

"Mom, we come from different times. Pretty isn't bad."

Her hand moved through the air as though she were swatting a gnat. She clearly didn't buy it. "Whatever. In my day it was not a good thing."

Dad walked in then and he knew something was up.

Mom jumped in and said, "Dear, what would you say if I called you pretty?"

"I'd ask you how much you had to drink." He set the bag filled with barbecue containers on the counter and stared at her. "I'm saying don't ever call me pretty. Why'd you say such a heinous thing?"

Mom turned to me and said, "See. Point made."

"Yeah, but y'all are old."

Now I'd done it. I insulted my parents.

"Old my ass," Dad said. "I'll remember that the next time you need money for something." Then he mumbled, "Old," and went for the plates.

We fixed our plates and ate in silence. When we were finished, Dad wanted to know how the pretty conversation came up. Mom told him, so he wanted to see Oliver. I showed him and he agreed that Oliver was very handsome, but definitely not a pretty man. From that day forward, I never referred to him as pretty in front of Mom and Dad.

Thanksgiving was the usual meal, but in all honesty, my mind was elsewhere—at Oliver's house, thinking about what he was doing. I didn't even mind all the noise at my aunt's. We made small talk, and I answered their questions about my job, but Dad, in his usual way, did the *eat and run*.

Thirty minutes after we finished dessert, and after all the dishes were in the dishwasher, Dad herded us to the car.

"Thank you for a lovely time," he said as he dashed out.

"Yes, it was fun." I waved as he practically dragged me to the car.

When we backed out of the driveway, I asked, "Dad, are you okay?"

"Hell, no, I'm not okay. I need a stiff drink. I don't

know what the hell my brother was thinking. I couldn't stand the noise any longer."

Mom patted his shoulder as we drove home. When we got there, he ran out of the car and into the house. By the time Mom and I got inside, he'd already downed a glass of bourbon. Damn, he really didn't like going there.

Chapter 5

MICHELLE

Oliver Facetimed me on Friday morning wondering when I was returning to the city. My initial reaction was to ask him why he even cared. Instead, I told him it would be the next morning.

"I miss you, Michelle. That little butt plug is staring at me right now."

My anger quickly melted into a series of giggles. "And why is that?"

"It's sitting in my hand, asking about your butt." He held up his hand and showed me.

"You're so bad."

"So how was Thanksgiving?"

When I told him about how Dad hightailed it out of noisyville, he cracked up.

"Sounds like your dad didn't have much fun."

"None at all. I'm sure he's already dreading Christmas."

Then he said, "Look." He angled the phone down and his cock was in his hand.

"Oliver, are you doing the dirty while you're on the phone with me?"

"Of course. I miss you so much, little Gumdrop. Every time I think of you, I get a fucking boner." Then he broke into the melody of, "It's Not Easy to be Me."

"You did not just sing that, did you?" I giggled again.

"Uhhh, yeahhh," he moaned. He switched the phone back so I could see his face. His lips dropped to the half-closed position and he licked them.

All my humor dissolved into desire. "Are you going to finish this off and let me watch?"

"Ohh yeah."

His hand slid up and down, up and down. He was naked, I only now realized. As I watched, my sex heated to the point where I had to slide my hand between my legs. When his hand pumped faster, mine rubbed to the same beat. Shit, this was hot.

"Talk to me. Show me where your hand is."

I moved the phone so he could see.

"Get rid of those damn underwear and open up that pussy for me. I want to see."

I tugged off my panties, one handed, and opened my legs wide.

"That's it. Pretty. So fucking pretty. Now rub yourself. I'd ask you to use two hands, but I'd lose sight of you and that just wouldn't do."

He was handling himself like a pro, pumping faster, the full length of his beautiful dick, stopping at the tip to put pressure on the head. I said, "I wish I could suck you off right now."

"Ah, me too."

He reached down for his balls and squeezed for a second and went back to the pumping action. Then he worked himself hard, and so did I.

I was so close, when creamy jets of cum shot in the air, spurting onto his abs.

"Now your turn." A couple of minutes later, I got mine, breath coming as hard as my spasms. My pussy soaked my hand and right about that time, Mom walked in.

"Michelle, when do you want to go to breakfast?"

I yanked up the covers as soon as I heard the doorknob turning. "Whenever. I need to shower first though."

"Okay. Dad and I will be waiting for you when you can be ready."

Then she was gone. I picked up the phone and Oliver was cracking up.

"Did Mom catch you rubbing the bean, babe?"

"Jeez. Not quite, but close. I better start locking my door here. I gotta go. We're going to breakfast. I'll call you later."

The day flew by with lots of food and visits with relatives, and on Saturday morning, I was headed back to Atlanta. Oliver was waiting for me at my house when I arrived. He helped me carry my bag inside and we decided to stay at home to watch a movie.

"How was your family?" I asked.

"The usual. Lots of food, and then I drove back here. Thanksgiving isn't that big of a deal for us."

"I see. What about Christmas?"

"What about it?"

"Is it a big deal?"

"Oh, yeah, I suppose. Like everybody else."

He didn't seem overly excited to discuss it, so I let it linger in the air for a second before I went on. "Are you spending it with them?"

He gave me an odd look. "Why do you ask?"

"Curious, I guess."

"Where else would I spend it?"

"I don't know."

"Are you inviting me to spend it with you?" he asked.

That had never crossed my mind, but now that he asked, it sort of looked that way.

"I'm not sure your parents would want you to."

"They wouldn't care. I see them a lot anyway."

Now I needed to check with Mom. "I have to clear it with my mother, but you'd be okay with that?"

"Yeah, I'd love to be with you on Christmas."

His emphatic answer had my excitement building.

"Maybe we could go to your parents' early on Christmas Eve and then leave for my parents'. That way we could kill two birds."

He glanced away and said, "Nah, my mom and dad really don't care. Besides, it's you I'm interested in."

"Oliver, are you ashamed of me?" The question popped out before I had a chance to think.

"What?" His confusion was as clear as glass.

"Is that why you won't take me to meet your family?" There, now it was out in the open and he couldn't avoid it any longer.

"Oh, God, no. Is that what you think?"

"Yeah. You go home all the time and never offer to bring me with you. Even on Thanksgiving you didn't extend an offer. Why wouldn't I think that?"

He scratched his head then ran a hand through his hair. Then he placed his hands on my shoulders. "I'm not, nor would I ever be, ashamed of you. It's more like I'm ashamed of them. They're a little weird to be honest. My sister dates a strange guy that none of us like, my parents don't believe in alcohol in any form, and the whole situation is a mess. I'd rather not expose you to that if at all possible."

"Why didn't you just say so in the first place?"

He shrugged. "It's not fun having a weird family. It's kind of embarrassing, especially when you talk about your parents and how cool they are."

"If you would've been at my aunt and uncle's house for Thanksgiving, you would've thought my family was strange too. Everyone has crazies when it comes to family, believe me."

"Maybe, but I don't really like to talk about them."

"Okay, I get it."

"So where's Sheridan? I thought she'd be here."

"She actually went on a little holiday."

"That's cool. We should do that sometime."

"Yeah, we should."

"I'd love to take you someplace. You deserve a little vacation. Well actually, you deserve a long one. You work so hard."

"Thank you, but you work hard too. We both should take a break."

"I don't tell you this enough, but I'm really proud of you. You've done so well in your job and I see how it excites you, Michelle."

"That really means a lot to me." And it did.

"I . . . I think you are the . . . you're really special to me."

I slipped my hands around his neck. "You're really special to me too."

"Since we can't take a vacation now . . ." His brows wiggled. "How about a little striptease in the meantime?"

"Like right now?"

He looked pointedly at my chest, and then down lower. "No time like the present."

Oliver took my hand and drew me to my feet.

"Do you need me to start this off?"

"Some music might help."

The next thing I knew, a sultry tune was playing and my top was off. My bra and thong followed and I swayed my hips. Wherever those moves came from, I had no idea. I'd always danced, but not like this. I bent over at the waist, dropped my head, then threw it back letting my hair fly. My hand traveled over my naked body, touching myself until he took over, saying he needed to do the rest. And he did a mighty fine job of it.

The rest of the night was one serious fuck fest, as Oliver demonstrated his artful mastery in that field. When morning came, I was delightfully sore in all the right places. He said I wasn't allowed to go out of town again without him. I guess that meant he was coming with me to my parents' for Christmas.

Chapter 6

MICHELLE

CHRISTMAS WAS AROUND THE CORNER AND I HAD PLANNED for Oliver to come home with me. Even Mom and Dad thought he was coming . . . until he dropped the bomb. That was what I got for assuming.

"When you said I wasn't allowed to go out of town again without you, I assumed that meant for Christmas. I even told my parents you'd be coming." He dipped his chin and slumped. At least he scored points for looking guilty.

"I'm so sorry. My mom and dad are insistent I spend Christmas with them."

I blew out a frustrated lungful of air. "But you said they wouldn't care." A long overdue argument was brewing and had been over this family issue. Better to get it out now than later.

He ran his hand through his perfectly messed thatch of hair and glanced up at the ceiling. He must've thought there were answers hiding somewhere in the heating vents. Or maybe there was a house elf like Dobby that would swoop in and save him. Silence greeted me and then expanded to an uncomfortable level in the room.

"Well?" I finally asked.

"I don't know what I can say to make you happy."

"You can start with the truth. Just tell me why you don't ever take me to meet your family." By now I was pissed. He had to know it too, as if my crossed arms and tapping foot didn't tip him off.

"I already told you. They're weird."

He shifted on his feet as he stared at me. I gave him some credit though. Drilling him with my gaze, he didn't so much as flinch a muscle. This lasted much longer than I expected. Eventually I told him to leave.

"You mean go home?"

"You can go anywhere you'd like. As long as it's not here," I said.

He looked like a cute little guppy for a few seconds, then backtracked. The hands started talking before the mouth. "Look, Michelle, it's not like I want to go. I would much rather spend the holidays with you."

"Then why don't you?"

"You know I would, but I don't want to anger them. You don't understand the dynamics of my family."

"Then explain it to me. I'm all ears." The thing was I would've listened to anything he had to tell me about them. But he never spoke of them unless I asked. "I asked you if you were ashamed of me, but you said you weren't. Are you ashamed of them?"

"N-not exactly. They're just different."

"Different. How?"

"Remember? They're sort of religious." He looked me straight in the eyes while he spoke so I had no reason to doubt him at the time. How I wished I had been more astute later.

"Religious? You never mentioned that before. And how is that a problem? Honestly, Oliver, you're always so nebulous when it comes to your family. I've got to say it's making me not trust you."

"I didn't mention it because I didn't want to worry you. They belong to a sort of religious cult."

"A religious cult."

"Uh, yeah. It's weird and my sister and brother do too. Every time I go there, they try to persuade me to join too. I'm afraid they'll put you on the spot to join too. I don't want to do that to you."

I wasn't buying it. There was something else there. "I'm not sure that's it. I think there's something else."

But he said, "Oh, baby, please don't worry about it. It's not what you think. I promise." Then he kissed me, swore to me everything was okay, and made me think all was right in our little world. Only deep in my heart I knew . . . I knew it wasn't. He made me forget it for a while. Before I knew it, we were back to status quo and on Christmas Eve, after a busy week at work, I climbed into my car and left for Mom and Dad's.

When I got home, I broke down and cried when Mom asked me where he was. It was more than a little embarrassing going into the explanation of why he didn't come. "I don't know what to think, Mom." Then I told her about the religion thing.

"Honey, I don't know what to tell you. But if he didn't care about you, why would he still be hanging around you?"

I didn't want to say it was because we fucked like rabbits all the time. My mother didn't need to hear that. Then she told me my aunt and uncle, along with the hellions, were coming over for our Christmas Eve celebration. I wanted to curl up like a shrimp in my bed and not socialize with anyone.

"Come on, honey, let's go spike the eggnog. I bought

those cute little moose cups and we'll get good and drunk tonight."

"Who's gonna cook if we do that?" I asked.

"Aww, who needs food anyway?" Then Mom laughed and I couldn't help laughing too.

Oliver didn't call that night nor did he text. My stubborn self wouldn't let me get in touch with him either. As I fell into bed, I thought about my present for him and how I'd planned on giving it to him in the morning. Well, too damn bad. He'd have to wait now, if I gave it to him at all.

Chapter 7

OLIVER

THE FLIGHT TO CHICAGO WAS OVERBOOKED, BUT I MADE IT in on time. Mom and Dad were eager to see me as I had missed the last two Christmases due to my crazy as hell work schedule. My sister and her husband were in town with their new baby. They lived in the burbs, only an hour away, so it wasn't that big of a deal for them to be here. Me, on the other hand, you would've thought I was the pope coming to town the way Mom acted.

"Oliver, you've changed."

"No, Mom, I'm your same old nerdy son."

"You were never nerdy. Only smart."

"You had blinders on, Mom."

She still did. Mom never saw how I hung out with all the geeks and was one myself. Even my pocket protector didn't give me away. I guess that's what's so great about moms. They only see what they want to see.

"So how's work? I do wish you would find that dream job of yours," she said.

"It's fine. I actually like it."

She wrinkled up her nose. "I don't know how you can.

Working on computers at a hospital. Whatever gave you the idea you should take that job?"

"The idea was a landing point until I found a better one, Mom."

She patted my shoulder like she had since I was five. "My Oliver deserves so much better."

I nodded and rushed up the steps to my room on the pretense of putting my bag up there. In reality, I wanted to escape the topic. If she only knew that I was an undercover agent for the Department of Homeland Security, she would have a massive freak the fuck out attack. That's why she thought I worked for a hospital maintaining their electronic medical records. With the way things were going on the Michelle front, I sometimes wished I were. She was poking into my personal life and the story I told her about my family was starting to burn a hole in my cover. Michelle wasn't stupid. She knew I was hiding something. The problem was I liked her. More than a whole fucking lot. The last thing I was supposed to do was get involved with someone. Everyone had warned me, but did I listen? Hell no. The reason was, I never thought it would amount to much more than a casual fuck every now and again. But dammit, I'd been so wrong. Every time I'd thought about ending things, an image of her on top of me, rocking her hips with my dick shoved deep in her pussy, came to mind, and no fucking way was I going to give that up to another man.

The truth was I had fallen for her . . . and hard. It had happened that night when she was dancing with her roommate. Long silky dark hair that swayed in motion with her body set me walking in her direction and I didn't stop until I stood face-to-face with the gorgeous creature that she is. Ever since then, we'd spent almost every night together. When we hadn't, I'd woken up doing the five-knuckle shuffle, dreaming about fucking her. I have to say, my dick has been one happy dude since she sailed into my life.

Only now, things were on the down swing. I needed to figure this shit out before I lost the greatest thing that ever happened to me. I'd even toyed with the idea of telling her the truth about me. But what if she didn't believe me? Or worse yet, what if she somehow got hurt by it? I couldn't live with that. There had to be some happy median and I was going to figure it out.

Mom knocked on my door and poked her head inside.

"Deanna's here with the baby." Her voice was laced with a sigh that only a grandmother could breathe. She was so excited about that little girl. I couldn't blame her. It would be years before I gave her any grandkids. Best not to burst that little bubble of hers. She'd probably already bought tiny pocket protectors for the thing.

I heard my sister scream my name at the top of her lungs, so I tore down the steps like a mad man. If she continued to yell like that around her daughter, that child would need hearing aids before the age of two.

"Get your ass over here, you big goon." She passed the squirming baby to her husband, Randy, and held out her arms. I hugged the crap out of her and realized exactly how much I'd missed my family in that moment.

"Damn, you look pretty good for popping out a kid not too long ago."

"Yeah, but you should see my boobs. Right, Rand?"

"Leave me out of this brother-sister talk," Randy said.

"That's disgusting. Why would you mention your boobs to me?" I acted like I was gagging.

"But it's the truth. I can show you later when I breastfeed."

Now I was totally disgusted. Holding up my hand like I

was warding off evil, I said, "You have gone past what's socially acceptable. I'm your brother."

"It's breastfeeding. Get over it, you big geek."

"Bleh." I shuddered.

"You need to get into the current century. Anyway, here."

She grabbed the baby from her husband and handed her to me. I had no idea what to do with the thing.

"Jesus, Oliver. You're like a block of wood. Relax. She's not going to eat you or anything."

"Yeah, but what if she . . ."

"What if she what?" Deanna asked.

"You know. Pukes or poops."

"Then you get to clean it up."

"You're gross. When did you get to be so gross? The last time I saw you, you were prim and proper."

"Yeah, well, try pushing an eight-pound human out of your vagina and see what happens to prim and proper."

I looked at my brother-in-law and said, "Dude, you need to rein her in."

"Not happening, man. Been there, tried that. Epic fail."

I stood there and gaped at my sister. This was clearly not the same person I remembered. She used to be so shy and would barely even say any unmentionable word around me. I recalled one time Mom asked me to help fold clothes and Deanna nearly had a heart attack because I folded a pair of her panties. Now look at her. She was spouting off about her boobs and vagina.

Mom sprinted into the room and caught sight of me holding little Ariana. "Aww, look how sweet Ollie looks holding the baby."

"Uh, yeah, just say a prayer she doesn't vom all over me."

"Oliver. She's only a tiny thing. She can't help it. You used to throw up on me all the time." Mom looked at me with a stern expression. I immediately felt like I was an adolescent again.

"Jeez. Sorry. But this is all new to me." I gazed down at the tiny bundle in my arms and her face was all puckered up. She was kind of cute, I supposed, if you counted the squished up bald look as cute. She actually resembled an old man, but I didn't let my sister know that.

"Why are you looking at her like that?" Deanna asked.

"Like what?"

"Like something's wrong with her?"

"I was just checking her out. It's not often I get to look at a baby," I told her. They were kind of creepy looking now that I thought about it.

"Okay. At least she doesn't look like Mary Jo Carmichael's baby," my sister said.

"What does her baby look like?" I asked.

"You wouldn't believe it. It looks exactly like an old man."

I nearly dropped baby Ariana. "No way." Those were the only words that came to mind. I couldn't possibly tell her I'd been thinking the exact same thing about her own baby. She'd stab me in the eyes with one of Mom's cooking knives. Then I'd never work again, not to mention my family would disown me for thinking such awful things.

Mom grabbed the baby from me and started making squawking noises. "Mom, you don't need to act like a bird," Deanna said.

"I'm not. She likes it. Look."

Sure enough. Ariana had a lopsided grin on her face.

"That's just gas," Deanna said. "The doctor said at this age when they smile they have gas. She probably only farted."

Mom tickled Ariana's chin. "Deanna, she knows a sound she likes when she hears one."

But then the room filled with an awful smell and my sister said, "Told ya. Gas."

Babies were gross. There was no getting around it. Only it got worse. The smell, I mean.

"Deanna, honey, I think she needs to be changed."

My sister's expression changed from happy to one that looked like she cashed in on the lottery. "That's fabulous. Oliver can do it."

"What? No! I don't know the first thing about changing diapers."

Deanna clapped her hands while Mom shoved Ariana into my arms. "It's time you learned, Ollie. Besides, you need to bond with your niece."

Taking a quick glance around the room, I noticed my brother-in-law had conveniently disappeared. Fuck me. Deanna was on her knees, digging through a gigantic duffle bag that was decorated with flowers and butterflies. It had to belong to baby Ariana.

"What are you doing?" I asked her.

"Getting your supplies."

Supplies? I needed supplies to change a diaper? Don't I just whip off one and put the other on? Apparently, I was way off base on that one. My sister ripped out a whole shit load of stuff. Then she laid out some fancy blanket thing on the floor and told me to set the baby down on it.

As soon as I did, Ariana let out a cry that made me scream. That made her cry even louder.

"Why'd you go and scare her like that?" Deanna asked.

"She scared the shit out of me!"

"Don't curse around her. It might offend her."

"Oh, for Christ's sake, she's only eight weeks old."

"So? You don't know what they pick up at that age."

Ariana was still screeching so I patted her belly, trying to calm her down. Deanna told me I needed to get her outfit off so I could change her. I stared at it for a moment, trying to figure that one out. It was an all-in-one number, so I rolled her over hunting for the buttons.

"What are you doing?"

"Looking for the buttons," I said.

"Good lord, you are helpless. There are snaps along the legs," Deanna huffed.

"Well I'm sorry, miss know-it-all. I've never changed a diaper before, much less undressed a baby. How was I to know?"

"Um, maybe those little white tabs would've given it away."

Sure enough, along the legs were snaps, so I undid them and pulled the little cotton thing up to find—holy mother of all shits. The poop had leaked out of the diaper.

"UGH." I covered my mouth, ran out of the room, and didn't stop until I hit the backyard. That was the most disgusting thing I'd ever seen. How in the world a little baby could produce all that, I'll never know. I do know one thing—kids were not going to be high on my agenda, unless whomever I married would sign up for all diaper changes. If not, I would have to carry around a vomit bag with me.

I wonder if Michelle would be good with that. What the fuck. Why am I even thinking along those lines? And then it hit me. I was crazy ass in love with her. What a great time to figure that one out—after finding a load of crap in my niece's diaper. That's one thing that I'd never share with her. Some secrets are meant to be kept.

Chapter 8

MICHELLE

To say that Christmas was a letdown would be an understatement. Oliver and I talked a few times, but it didn't replace him being here. Mom saw it in my eyes as I got in the car. Her words were not to worry, that things would shape up for Oliver and me.

When I got home to an empty house, I wanted to feel sorry for myself. I wanted Sheridan to be there, and not in her new situation. But I didn't call or bother her. She deserved her slice of happiness, and I wasn't going to spoil it for anything.

Early the next day, I got up and went to work. I was busy catching up from the time away. Our summer ads were due and my boss was impatiently waiting for copy on a bathing suit line. I was slightly behind on it, so I went to work, drumming up some great ideas. When she read what I handed her, her eyes lit up because I incorporated sun safety in the bottom.

"Michelle, this is your best work ever. I think those few days off must've freshened up your creativity."

She walked out, with me telling her I'd send over the

files and she could give the graphic artist the go ahead. My head practically slammed the desk afterward. My creativity was in the dumpster and had been since Oliver couldn't be honest with me. Not to mention all I thought about was his mouth and dick, or how I didn't trust him. And now she tells me I'm wonderful. What was I supposed to think? Maybe I needed to get my head out of my butt and straighten out my act. The problem was I was in too deep with Oliver. Now that I admitted it, maybe I could do something about it. But what?

Thrumming my fingers on my desk, there wasn't a solution in sight. Every time I brought up his little issue, he dodged the bullet and twisted me around his finger. What happened to my backbone? I could either accept things as they were or break it off entirely. Was I ready to do that? That was the question that had to be answered.

When I pulled in front of the house after work, his car was already there, waiting on me. He stepped out, holding a big Christmas gift bag.

I offered him a cool hello, but it didn't deter him one bit. Before I could unlock the front door, the bag was sitting on the porch, and I was in his arms, kissing him back, needing him as though he were the oxygen necessary to sustain life. In some ways, I felt he was. What the hell was wrong with me? What if he didn't have those same feelings in return?

He rested his forehead against mine. "I missed you, Gumdrop, more than I can say. I know you're still upset with me that I didn't go home with you for Christmas. How can I make it up to you?"

Even though the December night was chilly, his warm kisses had heated me up. How could he make it up to me? I didn't quite know how to answer him. So I only shrugged.

"I missed you too, Oliver. Let's go inside."

"Yes, so I can give you your presents."

"How was your family?"

Was it my imagination or did he just stiffen at my question? This was why I didn't trust him.

"Everyone was fine. Mom and Dad were their usual odd selves. How about yours?"

"Everyone was great. Dad dreaded Christmas."

I told him about my little cousins. "They're loud, obnoxious, and I'm almost certain they're bullies. The way they treat their younger siblings, it's hard not to miss it. My aunt and uncle do nothing about it. Dad gets so angry."

Then he told me that he was bullied in junior high and high school.

"You were?" That shocked me. He's so attractive. I couldn't imagine anyone bullying Oliver.

"Michelle, look at me. I mean really take a good hard look. I'm a geek. Geeks get picked on. I was a gamer, a computer nerd. I wasn't cool, didn't play sports."

When he put it like that, I imagined he was picked on.

"But your size. Usually kids bully the smaller ones."

"You are living under a rock. That is not true. Anyone is fair game, as long as they give the bullies something to latch onto. I did because I was the one in class who actually loved math, the sciences, chemistry, physics." Then he added the bit about wearing a pocket protector and I got it.

"I would've defended you."

"I don't think so."

"Oh, yeah I would have." I explained how when Sheridan's mom died everyone shunned her because they didn't know what to say, I stuck up for her. She was made an outcast and I wasn't having anything to do with that. "I totally would've stuck up for you. I hate that bullying crap."

"Wow. I didn't know that about Sheridan. You really did her a solid by staying her friend."

"A solid? I did what any friend should do. I did the right thing is all."

"Michelle, most people are like sheep and follow the herd. You are obviously a leader."

"I don't know about that. I only try to stand up for what's right."

He brought the Christmas bag over to me and we sat down. "Here. I hope you like everything."

"Thank you, but you didn't have to do this."

"Of course I didn't. But I wanted to."

The first item I pulled out was a giant stuffed pink gumdrop. I laughed.

"Just for you. It's your namesake," he said.

"Why do you call me that?"

"It's always been my favorite candy. Soft, sweet, and tasty. You remind me of one. They're the best things ever."

"Aww, thank you." I leaned over to kiss him. It was the cutest gumdrop in the world and had a big smile on its face. Next I pulled out an oblong box. When I unwrapped it, inside I found that little purple butt plug we never used and wrapped around it was a pretty gold bracelet. "Oh, look. The butt plug has jewelry now. Will my butt be all sparkly when I use this?"

He smirked and said, "Yes it will, but from sparks, not from that bracelet. That will be on your wrist. Let me help you put it on."

It was a simple gold bangle that had light etching on it and a basket weave pattern.

"It's so pretty. Thank you. I love it."

"You're welcome. Keep going."

"There's more?"

"Of course."

I was feeling bad because I didn't get him that much. I dug my hand into the bag and pulled out some sexy thongs. Yeah, very sexy, with lace and ties in the back.

"Oooh. Pretty."

"Yes. Keep going."

The next thing I pulled out was a box labeled *Womanizer Pro W500 Deluxe.* "What is this?"

A lopsided grin appeared on his face. "Open it and find out."

When I did, I laughed. "Santa must've been the naughty one this year."

"He was."

It was some kind of an air vibrator you held over your clit.

"I did some research and we're going to use it in conjunction with the butt plug."

"We are?"

"Well, that's if you're willing." His face was eager with anticipation. The truth was, I was more than curious about the tiny plug. It wasn't much bigger than my pinky, so it didn't look very intimidating at all. Everything I read about anal seemed positive when it was done right, so why not.

"Just wait. I'll have you screaming before the night's over." It didn't take much for me to get aroused when I was with Oliver, so I was confident he was right.

We eventually made it to my bedroom after I gave him his gifts—which consisted of a picture of the two of us taken at the Halloween party in a frame I had made and then I bought him a really cool print of a collage of all kinds of computers dating back to the early seventies. It was huge in a modern black frame. He absolutely went crazy over it. His appreciation began with a slow, sensual kiss, which soon escalated into one of passion and lust. That was how we ended up racing up to my bedroom, frantically ripping each other's clothing off in the process.

He pulled out the Womanizer, which at first made me giggle, but he placed the little cup over one of my nipples and turned the thing on. I nearly ended up on the ceiling.

"Jesus. What's in there?"

"Air. Suction. Just wait until we test it on your clit."

Then he dove for my other nipple as I reached for his already stiff cock. It had been longer than I cared to remember that we had been without each other. He was as smooth and hot as ever and I wanted him inside of me. But he had other plans in mind.

He took the new toy off my nipple and moved it to my clit, positioning it just right. Well I'll be damned. It felt like his mouth had formed a suction over it and was going to town. I gave a little jolt as he turned up the intensity. But he wasn't finished. He put my hand on top of the toy and told me to hold it in place, like I would argue with that. Before he could do much of anything, I was moaning out my first orgasm.

"That was the fastest climax I've ever had." I held the little device up to inspect it. There really wasn't anything to see.

"You came that fast?" he asked.

"Uh, yeah. It was intense too."

"Well, get ready for more."

He lubed up the little plug and slowly inched it inside my puckered hole. By now I was curious and the sensation was different—not anything that I expected. He grabbed my new favorite toy and placed it back over my clit, turned it on, and then moved the plug a little. Now the sensations changed into something entirely different. I was already close to coming and with that back door occupied, in no time at all, I was yelling out his name, exactly like he'd predicted. I felt so full, in a good way, as my blood raced, every nerve ending firing at the same time. This was one orgasmic trip he was taking me on.

"Keep holding that on your clit."

My breathing was uneven as I watched him roll on a condom and take his hard dick into his hand. My gaze dipped lower to where he slid into my wet and ready pussy, not slow but fast. Now I was stretched, with the plug still inside of me as well. I panted his name as he just sat there, wanting more.

"How do you feel?"

He expected me to have a little chat with him now? I could barely breathe, much less talk.

"G-good."

"Is that all?"

"N-no. J-just fuck me. I need you to move."

A throaty laugh hit my ears, but I didn't care. All I did care about was feeling him pumping deep within me. The motion of his cock against that butt plug was fucktastic.

And then he began, slow at first, but he must've read my mind as I arched my back to meet him. Hooking his arms under my knees, he picked up speed and went all out. Each time he slammed into me all the way, he hit the plug and it sent a series of tremors racing through me. I finally had to let that little toy go because my hands lost their dexterity and I couldn't hang onto it any longer.

"Ahhh," I moaned. He swiveled his hips, then ground them against me, putting pressure on the plug and that was it. Another intense climax had me shooting to the moon. I saw stars, maybe even blacked out. It might've been from lack of oxygen. I heard him groan and knew somewhere in the back of my mind that he came too. When he bit down on a nipple, it brought me back to the present and I focused on him again.

"Jeez, you must be trying to kill me or something."

"Hardly. I'm pleasuring you."

"I'll say."

"You liked it, I assume?"

"I'm pretty sure the neighbors know I liked it."

"They might." His tongue tickled my neck and then he reached for the little butt plug. "So this was a win then?"

"Oh, yeah. I didn't think it would be though."

"I want to get you one with a little tail and see you walk around in it."

"What are you talking about?" Then he explained that they make them with a tail attached. "I think I'll pass on that."

"What about wearing this to a party?"

"Not a chance."

"You can always take it out if you don't like it."

"Nope. Not gonna happen. Have you always been into kink like this?"

"Only you. You make me this way. Seeing you aroused makes me so fucking hard." He nipped at my neck and I shivered.

"So how did you learn about all this stuff?"

"I Googled it. And it's only one little butt plug. Anal is really popular, you know."

"I guess I did, but I've never done it."

"I know. Well, I didn't really *know* know, but I figured because you would've been more . . ."

"More what?"

"Open."

"I'm open."

"Yeah, that's not what I meant. More knowledgeable."

"Okay, I'll go with that."

"So no chance of you wearing this to the party, then?"

"No way! And what party?"

He nudged me. "Friday. Zack and I are throwing our After Christmas Holiday party, remember?"

I slapped my forehead. He mentioned something about that before Christmas, but I forgot about it.

"You invited Sheridan and Beck, didn't you?" he asked.

"Yeah, I just need to shoot her a text to remind her. But I'm too tired now. And we haven't eaten dinner."

"I'll order a pizza now and we can eat in bed." He grabbed his phone and placed the order. I was so exhausted I didn't move until the doorbell rang. When I went to get up, he pointed a finger at me. "You stay put. I'll be right back." He tugged on his jeans and ran downstairs to pay the delivery guy.

A little bit later he showed up with the pizza box, two plates, two bottles of beer, and some napkins.

"You're talented to carry all that. You must've waited tables before."

"Sure did. In college. It was at a pizza place, in fact."

"That's why you're so handy." And then I realized what I said and laughed. "Maybe working there made you really good in bed too."

"I hope not. It was a terrible place to work. And their pizza sucked."

We dove into our dinner and were too hungry to talk for a few. Then I asked him about the party. He said it would be a repeat of the Halloween one.

"You know, the same crowd only no costumes this time."

"Oh, cool. Just let me know if I can bring anything."

"Actually, I was going to ask for your help with the appetizers. I'm having some of it catered. Deli trays and things like that. Would you mind too much making some dips?"

"Not at all." I gave him a few ideas and as he stated, guys would eat anything. He was right about that.

After we ate, I got up to brush my teeth, and when I walked into the bathroom, the butt plug was on the sink.

"Um, Oliver, am I supposed to do something with that butt plug?"

He cracked up. "I already took care of that. I probably shouldn't have left it sitting there, but I forgot about it."

"Yeah, good thing I have my own bathroom."

"Michelle, you don't have a roommate anymore."

"Well, true, but you never know. What if my mom showed up or something?"

"Bring it to me and I'll keep it at my place."

The whole time I washed my face and brushed my teeth, I couldn't help but think how much I liked that little thing. I wondered if I was a deviant or something. When I came back out, I asked Oliver and he only laughed at me.

"As long as it feels good . . ."

Handing him the little thing, I said, "You can take this home, but I'm keeping the Womanizer."

"Does that mean if you don't answer the phone when I call, I can assume you have that thing attached to your clit?"

"Most likely."

"Just don't let it take the place of my mouth. I like licking your little button."

Then I laughed. "I can carry this thing in my purse, but your tongue is sort of attached to you."

"Good point."

He went to brush his teeth and I examined my new favorite toy. It was pretty stupendous. If I weren't so tired, I'd use it again. But that would likely cause a chain reaction leading to fucking and I had to get up in a little while. Oliver climbed back in bed and soon he was snoring lightly. I, however, was still awake. I kept staring at that Womanizer so I decided to put it to use. In less than two minutes, I orgasmed, curled up behind my guy, and fell asleep. I dreamed about a sexy guy with dark-framed glasses sucking on my clit all night.

Chapter 9

MICHELLE

IN THE MORNING, MY DREAM WAS REALITY. OLIVER'S HEAD was between my legs, which were raised and pushed up high, as he tongued his way all around my pussy. I moaned and pulled his hair, begging him to fuck me. He didn't. Not then anyway. After I came, he flipped me on my stomach and then slid into me, coaxing another climax out of me.

I glanced at the clock on the bedside table and yelled, "Oh, shit. I'm late." I flew into the bathroom. There wouldn't be time to wash my hair, only time for a quick rinse in the shower. I dry shampooed and dressed in record time. Oliver was still in bed.

"What are you doing?" I asked. "Don't you have to work?"

"Yeah. I'm late now. What're another few minutes? I'll take a shower, but I wanted to let you have the bathroom."

I shrugged, not having time to discuss this point. "I'll talk to you later. Lock up when you leave."

When I got to work, I was completely frazzled. My boss took one look at me and asked me if I'd had a rough night.

"Uh, I couldn't fall asleep until late and then I overslept."

"Michelle, is everything okay?"

"Fine, why?"

"You only have make-up on one eye."

"Oh, crap. I was in such a hurry I forgot."

"Um, I hate to be the bearer of bad news, but it sort of looks like you forgot your bra too."

I looked down to see my nipples through the shirt I had on. I had indeed forgotten my bra. What the hell was wrong with me? Thank God I brought a sweater. It was always freezing in the office, which was why my nips were trying to poke through my shirt.

"Oh, God." My head dropped down. "I'm such a dork."

She laughed and patted my shoulder as I put on my sweater and buttoned it up.

"It could be worse. At least you have a sweater."

"If I didn't, I'd wear my coat all day," I huffed. "Now I have to figure out what to do about my naked eye. I don't have any eyeliner or mascara with me."

She grabbed my arm and said, "Come with me. I've got you covered." She kept extra make-up in her desk drawer. "I'm always having to go to some meeting after work and never have time to go home."

"You're a lifesaver."

"Just keep those." She eyeballed them for a second, then said, "They've never been used."

"You're sure I can have these?" I asked.

"Yep. They're yours."

I decided to keep them in my desk in case I did anything this stupid again. Maybe I should keep a bra in there too. Oliver really had messed up my morning. When

I got to my desk, I texted him to let him know. I wasn't surprised by his response.

You just made my day. It was followed by a series of laughing emojis.

———

THE DAY of Oliver's party arrived and I was super busy making appetizers. I generally enjoyed cooking, but wasn't exactly an expert. The kitchen was a disaster with mixing bowls and measuring cups everywhere. Two of the appetizers had to be baked. One was an artichoke parmesan dip and the other was a buffalo chicken one, so I decided to bake them at Oliver's. The other two were cold and they were ready and waiting in the refrigerator. Now all I had to do was clean up and shower.

After I was dressed, I loaded up the car and headed to the guys' house. They had already moved the furniture, had the bar set up, the music was playing, and the table was ready for the food. All they needed was to set up for the buffet. They had purchased plates, utensils, napkins, and cups, which were all in the kitchen, so I went about getting those out, after I stuck the dips in the oven. Guests would be arriving in about forty-five minutes. The catered food soon arrived and was set up and my appetizers were ready.

It was great to catch up with Sheridan and Beck. They said their Christmas was awesome. Apparently English got a puppy and named it Boonior (which was a combination of her dog Boonie that died, and junior) and the thing was cute as hell, but ate socks and slippers and pooped everywhere. They had me dying laughing with the stories.

Oliver came up to us and stole me away to introduce me to his work associates.

"But I thought I met them at the Halloween party."

"You did, but I wanted to make sure you remembered them since they all had costumes on."

"Ahh, good point."

He rattled off a bunch of names I recalled. They were outside around the fire pit again, but no one seemed to be able to keep the fire going.

"Let me see if Beck can." I went back inside to grab him and Sheridan. His fire building skills came through and soon there were roaring flames warming the group of us out there.

Oliver announced, "Don't forget to eat, everyone. We have a ton of food inside."

Tara, one of Oliver's co-workers, sidled up to me and asked a bunch of questions about Oliver and me. It was a little strange and I got the impression that maybe she had an interest in him. But then I was distracted by Sheridan and forgot about it. Tara kept approaching me, asking me things such as how close I was to Oliver or how often Oliver and I saw each other. She was super friendly and not catty at all. I finally asked her if she had an interest in him and she laughed it off, saying they were only work friends. I told myself I would mention it to Oliver later, but time and alcohol made me forget about it.

Later, I noticed him talking to Tara and it appeared they were arguing. I wondered about that, but Zack's girl-friend grabbed me because she was on the hunt for more tortilla chips. Then Sheridan and Beck were leaving so I walked out front with them to say goodbye.

"It was great seeing you. Let's not take this long before we get together again," I said.

"I know. It's crazy busy with a little one, though," she said.

"Not to mention work." She wiggled her fingers as they walked to their car.

When I went back inside, I couldn't find Oliver. I asked Zack and he said they were out back, so I headed that way. As I walked out the door, the loud conversation hushed. This wasn't the first time it happened. Did his work friends not like me? I was going to find out.

"Hey everyone. Do I smell bad or something?"

Oliver cracked up. "Why would you ask that?"

Sweeping my arm out in a wide arc, I said, "Because every time I walk out here, y'all stop talking."

He rushed up to me and said into my ear, "That's because you're so fucking hot."

"Oh, come on Oliver, it's the truth. I'm getting a complex around your work friends. It's super awkward."

He steered me away from the group and the porch light reflected the true concern in his expression. His brows were drawn together and even though he wore his glasses, they didn't conceal it. There were several more creases on his forehead, so I reached up to smooth them out.

"I don't want you to feel that way. We weren't talking about you. We were discussing a work issue. No one wants to bore you with our work speak."

"I don't mind you talking about work, but to go quiet is strange to me."

"It's not because of you. They don't want to talk over your head about computer shit, you know?"

He cupped my cheeks when I didn't respond and said, "Michelle, tell me it's good. I don't want your feelings hurt."

What to say to that? He'd hurt my feeling before, with all the avoidance about going to his parents' house, but I'd kept my mouth shut time and again. This wasn't the time or place for this discussion. So I only nodded. Unfortunately, that got my wheels spinning again, which I wish it hadn't.

"What's wrong?" he asked.

"Nothing."

"Don't lie."

"Oliver, I get the feeling you're the one who lies to me all the time."

Large blue eyes grew even larger. "Why would you say that?"

My expression said, *Come on, Oliver, you know why.*

He didn't say another word. We stared at each other but it felt like we were miles apart. Suddenly, he blurted out, "Michelle, I'm in love with you. Nothing is what you think."

"What's that supposed to mean?"

He rubbed his face and shook his head. "It's . . . there's more to it."

"Then tell me."

"I can't. But I will soon. Please, trust me."

I didn't want to hear any more weird stories or excuses, so I walked inside. I went to the front closet where I had put my purse and headed out the front door. No one noticed, as they were all engaged in conversations with various people. As I got in my car and drove to my house, which was less than a mile away, I wondered how long it would take for Oliver to call.

My phone rang as the words drifted in my head. I ignored it. It wasn't until I got home that I answered it. It was the fifth time he'd called.

"Where are you?" His voice was frantic.

"Home."

"Why did you leave?"

"You seriously have to ask that? I know in my heart

you're not being honest with me. You're hiding something from me and I can't deal with it."

"Listen to me. I love you."

"Love isn't enough, Oliver, when deceit is involved."

A heavy sigh hit my ears. "You don't understand."

"Then explain it to me. I'm not an idiot. I may not be a member of Mensa like you and your friends are, but I can comprehend most things." My jab was cutting as it was meant to be. I was tired of being treated like . . . well, I didn't exactly know what.

"That's not fair."

"Yes, it is. Your work friends look at me like I'm not welcome. I don't like it and don't want to be around them anymore."

"They don't—"

"They do. You're not paying attention if you think anything else. Or you're blind and deaf if you don't see how they treat me and whisper behind my back. But I do."

"It's not what you think."

"As I've asked you before, tell me. But you seem incapable of that. So at this point, I believe we should end this conversation before it escalates into something ugly." And that's what I did. My phone rang several more times and then it dinged with texts, which I ignored. Instead, I washed my face, brushed my teeth, and curled up in bed with my pillow, trying to figure out why my sexy geek of a boyfriend refused to explain his mysterious life to me.

Chapter 10

OLIVER

DAMAGE CONTROL. THAT'S WHERE I WAS HEADED. TARA grabbed me after my phone conversation with Michelle and wanted to know what was wrong. When I told her, she said it was for the best. My reaction was horrific. I wanted to jam my fist through her face—but I didn't. I stared at her as though she were Medusa standing in front of me.

"What?" she asked.

"How can you say that? Michelle is the sweetest, most beautiful person I know."

"She'll ruin this op if you're not careful, and then what'll you do?"

"Walk away from this job, that's what."

"You can't do that and you damn well know it."

That was the second time I wanted to slam my fist through her face in less than a minute.

"You can be a cold, heartless bitch."

"So I've been told." A smile didn't accompany her words. "We've been working on this for close to eighteen months and you're ready to walk because of a woman who can't listen to you and know her place."

My hands fisted and I crammed them into my pockets before I did something really stupid. I was not a violent guy by nature, but Tara was pissing me off. Her callous approach to Michelle was over the top and I wasn't going to stand for it.

"Know her place? Let's get one thing straight. Michelle has a place—a very important one—in my life. Get used to it, Tara. She won't be pushed to the back any longer. This idea of her knowing her place is archaic. She has no idea of what's going on. And what if someone said that about you?"

"Well, I wouldn't put myself in that position."

My jaw hit the floor. "How can you be so sure?"

"I just wouldn't." She walked away. It was a good thing. I was tired of this conversation. Tara grated on my nerves and I could only handle her in small doses. The fact that we worked so close on a daily basis was bad enough, but now the friction between us had grown to an intolerable level. The other guys had mentioned it and I reined in my nasty comments as much as I could. She was good—one of the best agents if I was honest. But sometimes being good didn't compensate for being a giant bitch.

I found myself pacing, trying to formulate a plan because Michelle wasn't answering the phone. And when she did, our conversation went to shit. I didn't blame her. I had made her feel small and who wanted that? If she had done the same to me, I would've walked a long time ago. She had given me every opportunity in the world to open up, and I didn't. But how could I without revealing the truth? I didn't want to put her in any danger.

For whatever reason, when I was around her, I stumbled when it came to telling her about my personal life. It made me sound like a liar and then I had to cover my tracks and it made it even worse, which was why I always diverted her with sex. Don't get me wrong, sex with Michelle was awesome. It was better than anything I could imagine. But that proverbial rock and hard place were crushing me at the present time, and I didn't know how to handle it. The real problem was, I had fallen madly in love with her and didn't want to lose her. No, it wasn't part of the plan. No, I wasn't supposed to do it. But who in the fuck ever plans to fall in love? I certainly hadn't.

Zack came in and saw me.

"Hey, dude, what's wrong? You look like your dog just died."

"Yeah, I wish it were that easy."

"What's the problem?" he asked.

"Michelle."

"Ah. What are you gonna do?"

"I may not have to do anything. She got tired of the game. She won't even talk to me now."

"Yeah, I got a vibe the last time she came outside and we all stopped talking."

"Why the fuck did you do that?"

"Dude, we were talking about work. What were we supposed to do?"

"Keep talking, just change the topic. She thought you were talking about her, you fucktard. And now Tara is on my ass too."

"Fuck Tara. She acts like she owns this mission."

I shrugged. "I'm going to bed. You can clean up."

"Sorry, man. I really am."

I ignored him and climbed the stairs to my bedroom, where her scent lingered in the air. How could everything turn south so quickly? One minute everything was great and the next . . . bam. That wasn't quite true. This had been brewing for a while. I had just been pushing it back in my head, hoping for a better resolution. All I knew was I needed to get my girl back or I would never be a happy guy.

Chapter 11

MICHELLE

OLIVER CALLED THE NEXT DAY AND I fiNALLY ANSWERED.

"Michelle, are you okay?"

"Yes, no. No, Oliver, I'm not okay."

"Can I come over?"

"What purpose would that serve?"

"We need to talk."

"About what? You won't tell me anything."

"Look, there are things."

"What things? If you can't be upfront with me, I don't think we should see each other anymore. I can't deal with being involved with you if I can't trust you. Right now I have no trust in you."

"Please, Michelle. Don't do this."

"Oliver, you have it backward. You're the one that's doing it. Not me. Be honest with me and things will be fine. But until you can open up to me, I can't find it in my heart to stay in this relationship. Goodbye, Oliver."

I pushed the end button and sat staring at my phone. A text came in from him immediately.

Please don't do this.

I didn't respond.

———

A COUPLE of weeks passed since that night and my decision was made. More than anything, I needed to find out where the hell Oliver spent his time. If he loved me—and I truly thought he did and I loved him too—I wanted to know what in the world was going on. That was what pushed me to purchase the GPS device to go on his car. I could not believe I was being this snoopy. If any boyfriend of mine had ever done anything like this, I would've dumped him in a skinny minute. I guess it didn't matter because Oliver and I weren't really seeing each other anymore. Still, out of curiosity, I wanted to know where he went.

Another week passed by before I got up the nerve to actually put the damn thing on his car. One night, after midnight, I drove by his house. All the lights were out and his car was parked out front. I went down the street a ways, got out, and ran to the vehicle. Then I placed the small device under the front left fender near his tire, exactly like the instructions described. As soon as it was securely in place, I scooted the hell out of there.

When I was home, I opened up the app on my phone and sure enough, it was activated and beeping in the exact location of his home address. I hadn't told anyone I was going to spy on my ex-boyfriend. I felt like some creepy peeping tom, but whatever. I had to know. And that was that.

For five solid days I checked the app like some kind of possessed woman. It got to the point where I was acting stupid over it. So I decided to not pay attention to it anymore.

That lasted an entire week until Oliver called out of the blue and we had a nice chat. His voice brought all the feels back and then I felt guilty about having that device stuck on his car. I almost told him about it so he could hate me forever and take the damn thing off. But instead I began tracking him again.

It was early February and unseasonably warm. I was itching for spring and sick of winter. My life was a sad mess. I was lonely without Oliver. He started calling again occasionally, yet never answered the pointed questions I asked. He stuttered and then changed the topic every time. My heart broke after each conversation so I chose to avoid them altogether.

Friends at work were tired of my moping and suggested I date someone else. Even Sheridan was getting a little tired of it. But the thought of being with someone else didn't go over well. Every time someone would point a guy out, my response was always the same. He wasn't as sexy as Oliver. Or he wasn't as smart as Oliver. Or he wasn't as tall as Oliver. Or I didn't like the way he dressed. Oliver was more hip. Or he didn't wear sexy glasses like Oliver. I was hopelessly, madly in love with a man who was as mysterious as the true identity of Jack the Ripper. That's how I got back on board with the tracker device.

The rest of the week passed with nothing unusual. He went to work every day, then back home. He made a few side trips here and there to the grocery store, his favorite sports bar, and a couple other places such as friends' houses and the gym. Then on Sunday, he made a trip to the outskirts of a small town about an hour northeast of Atlanta. This must've been where his parents lived. He stayed there for several hours, and then came home. It didn't raise any red flags for me until he did it two more times—only those times he did it at eleven at night. Why would he go visit his parents so late at night, unless something serious had happened?

I decided I would give him a call the next day just to check in to make sure everything was all right. Since he didn't know I had my fingers on where he went every day, I had to make him believe I was in the dark.

"Michelle. This is an unexpected surprise," he said. He was the one who usually called me.

"A good one or a bad one?"

"Oh, a great one. I was sure you wouldn't call me again." He sounded genuinely happy to hear from me.

"Yeah, I know. I don't want to give you any false illusions though, Oliver."

"I wish you would give us another try."

"I can't until you open up to me. I know there's more and can't understand why you won't tell me." He was quiet for so long, I broke the silence. "So, how've you been?"

"Fine, other than missing you."

He didn't sound fine, but he said nothing about his parents. That raised an alarm. So then why did he go out there? And not only once but twice. I let it drop and didn't bring it up.

"Work okay?"

A soft sigh escaped him and my skin instantly pebbled with goosebumps. His voice, his breath, everything about Oliver was sexy. God I missed him and those dark-framed glasses. Why wouldn't he open up to me?

"Work is work. How about you? The last time we were together, you were swamped with the summer ads. Everything settled down now?"

"Pretty much." He was always so attentive to every part of my life. Except for the questions he wouldn't answer. "We're in the calm before the next storm."

"Which is?"

"Christmas," I said with a laugh.

"Jesus, it's not even spring."

"Right? But that's how far in advance we have to plan and bid for the jobs."

"Michelle, I miss the hell out of you. Not a day goes by when I don't think of you."

My gut twisted with his words. We were so happy when those shadows didn't pop out to get in the way. "I miss you too. I'd better be going."

"Take care of yourself, okay?"

"You too."

Melancholy nailed me as I thought about how I could be in his bed, under him, kissing him right now, if only . . . if only what? I knew what and it wasn't happening. That's why I was secretly stalking him. It scared me to think I had stooped to that level. And what would it accomplish? I knew he was going out late at night but I didn't ask him about it. So what was my next move?

That answer came the following Sunday. I was sitting at home in the evening, staring at the stupid app, when Oliver's car began to move. I had nothing better to do, so I decided to follow him. It was about seven o'clock at night. I was far behind him so he had no idea I would be following him.

Nearly an hour later, I pulled off the interstate and traveled down a winding road until the GPS indicated I needed to turn down a gravel road. He was really off the beaten path. When he said his family lived out in the sticks, he meant it.

A few miles later, I slowed to a crawl to eliminate the dust I was stirring up and switched my headlights to parking lights, even though it wasn't the smartest thing, but I didn't want him to find me out here, tailing him. As I rounded a curve, up ahead I saw a house sitting off the road. It was hard to miss, as it was the only one around. Oliver's car sat in the driveway, along with another one. I stopped and put my car in reverse, pulling it off to the side. Thank God my cell phone had that flashlight app on it or I would've been stumbling around in the dark.

I carefully picked my way around bushes and God knows what—I didn't even want to think what could've been slithering around my feet. When I got to the house, I crept around the windows, but couldn't get a good look inside—until I found a painter's bucket next to the front porch. Turning it upside down, I stepped up on it and peered through the blinds. My heart sank to my toes as I saw Oliver in the room talking animatedly with a woman. There was no family there. It was just the two of them. I was crushed. I could hear muffled words, but couldn't make anything out. She was gesturing with her hands, and he was paying close attention.

I was even more upset by how beautiful she was. She wore a baseball cap pulled low over her eyes, but she had a long blond ponytail and wore exercise clothing. Her long legs were endless, which made me even more depressed. I wanted to cry. He spun her around, her back toward me, and started fiddling with her shirt. Was he undressing her? Were they going to have sex? As I stared at them, it hit me. I knew her. It was Tara. They worked together. Oh my God! He'd been cheating on me with one of his co-workers.

The thought shocked me so much I lost my balance on the paint bucket and that's when the catastrophe hit. In my struggle to save myself, I grabbed the window ledge, which forced my head into the glass, causing a big thumping sound. Then I fell off the bucket, face first into the giant shrub that was there, getting tangled up in the thing. It wasn't exactly my most graceful move, I have to say. The motion set off the floodlights and, of course, Oliver and Tara came running outside.

When he discovered it was me lying head first in the bushes, he said, "Michelle, what the hell are you doing here?" He pulled me out of the stupid hedge.

"I might ask the same of you." Leaves and twigs were everywhere, but my face stung like fire. I wasn't sure if it was from embarrassment or if I had scratched the hell out of it. It felt like a little of both. My accusing glare ping ponged between my ex-boyfriend and his lover, and he actually had the decency to squirm.

"Michelle, this isn't . . . I mean we weren't . . ." He blew out a huff.

The other woman said, "You might as well tell her."

"Tell her?" he asked, his voice rising.

"Tell me what? That you've been screwing around on me? That's obvious," I said.

"That's not what we're doing here," he said. "Tara and I work together." His hands flew in the air and he held something in one of them that had a long wire attached to it. The wire flew around, nearly hitting him in the head.

"Indeed. We've met. Remember? I'm sure you get a lot of work accomplished. At least now I know where you go on all your *family* outings." Family my ass.

Then he informed me my face had blood on it. How more perfect could this be? I dabbed my fingers to it and held them up to the light. Sure enough, blood was present. "Great. Exactly what I need." I was done with him and this conversation. I started to walk away when he grabbed my arm.

"Where are you going?"

"Home." I pulled my arm away.

"No, you honestly don't understand. Tara and I . . . were working."

"You expect me to believe that?"

"No! I mean yes."

Shaking my head at him, I said, "You two need to get a better story than that. I'm out of here." I moved past him, but he grabbed my arm again.

"Michelle, I have to explain. Come inside. I can help you clean up your face. Besides, you don't understand. None of it. Tara and I work together but not in the way you think."

I aimed my finger at him. "See. I knew it. You two are together. Look, you've done enough damage already, Oliver. I thought I was important to you . . . meant something to you. But things never added up. Now I know why. The lies, the secrets. It all makes sense now. You and Tara. Well, I'm through with you. Now let me go."

This time when I tried to leave, he didn't stop me. But as I turned, he said, "I love you, Michelle, and it really isn't what you think."

"Yeah, tell that to your other girlfriend," I mumbled. I started to jog back to my car when my toe caught on something and I went sprawling. What the fuck else was going to happen to me? I scrambled to my feet as a thought hit me. "You know, if I'd caught you creeping around my house like this, I would've freaked. But you really haven't. That only confirms your guilt to me. And you didn't ask me a single question about how I found you. Now why is that, Oliver?"

He stared at me with his beautiful mouth slightly parted. Even after all this, all I wanted to do was kiss him. God, I hated myself right then. I limped away and by the time I got to the car, tears clouded my vision. Why did I have to fall for a guy who couldn't be faithful? Why couldn't I fall for someone who only wanted me? And why the hell did I stand on a stupid paint bucket of all things?

Chapter 12

OLIVER

If she drove away, I didn't stand a chance. I didn't give a shit that she figured out where I'd been going . . . that she spied on me. I wanted her in my life, so I sprinted to her car and knocked on the window. Her head rested on the steering wheel and it ripped me in two to see how broken she was.

"Michelle, at least let me in the car. I can explain, I swear to God I can. You can't drive home like this."

The tear-stained face that met my eyes held such anger I nearly jumped backward. Her window went down and she said, "How long has it been going on? I just want to know."

"Honestly, you're not getting it. There's nothing between us other than work. I swear it."

"Oh, come on, Oliver. Give it up already."

I ran around to the passenger door and was surprised to find it unlocked. Once I was seated, I started with my explanation.

"I couldn't tell you before . . . hell, I'm not supposed to tell you now. Tara and I are with Homeland Security. We work undercover investigating companies who we believe have been linked to cyber threats. That's why I wasn't able to reveal anything to you." He held up the little black thing and said, "I was showing her how to wear this wire when we heard you."

"Homeland Security. Undercover."

She wasn't buying it.

I reached into my back pocket and pulled out my credentials, which I rarely carried when I was working undercover. For some reason I had them with me, but couldn't explain why.

"Your name's not Oliver Griffith."

"No. Well, sort of. Oliver's my middle name and the one I prefer. But my full name is Griffin Oliver Baker. That's why the card says Griffin O. Baker. Oliver Griffith is my undercover name."

She held my badge and ID for a while, staring at them, running her fingers over them.

"Michelle, I couldn't tell you. Even now, it puts everything at risk."

"I don't understand."

"I know. The people running the company are dangerous. That's why we're undercover."

"But it's a computer company." She was resisting my explanation. I would've, too.

"That's right. But they're doing illegal things and we're on the cusp of breaking their operation open. It's taken us about eighteen months to infiltrate it and get to this point. If they find out that we're on the wrong side, they'll pack things up and be gone before we can nail them for everything."

She rubbed her face and flinched. In all this shit, she must've forgotten about the scratches on her cheek.

"Will you please come back inside so I can at least

clean off your face? And then maybe Tara can help explain all this. I swear to God we are not fucking nor have we ever been."

I was more than a little shocked to see her hand reach for the door handle. Then she got out and headed for the porch. I tagged along even though I wanted to grab and hug the shit out of her. When we walked inside, Tara grinned.

"I see you salvaged this mess."

Michelle spoke up, saying, "I want to hear the whole story. From both of you."

"This big jerk isn't supposed to get involved while he's on a job," Tara said.

I answered quickly. "This job's been going on for too long. Besides, when this woman entered my life, there wasn't anything that could've prevented me from getting involved with her. What I never expected was to fall in love."

"Yeah, well, good luck explaining that to Ren."

"Who's Ren?" Michelle asked.

"She's our ball-busting boss. And she'll be mad as hell at me for telling you all this, but too fucking bad. Now let's get your face cleaned up before you get an infection."

Afterward, Tara and I gave her a brief explanation of how each member of the team was hired by the company to do our respective jobs. Then after a time, when they figured they could trust us, they began asking us to do shady shit. I didn't give her all the details of how it started with small things, like tapping into accounts only to check balances, on the guise that they were clients. We knew they weren't, but we did as they asked. Then when they gave us more "responsibilities" and we didn't raise any flags, we built up their trust.

Now we'd gotten to where they had us hacking into

banking systems, healthcare systems—almost anywhere that stored social security numbers. To the average employee, they might think they were moving funds for a client, but we knew better. We had a detailed list of who their clients were and none of them required what they were having us do. This company was a den of cyber thieves. They buried the money in Swiss banks and then laundered it. We couldn't believe how wide their operation spanned and how deep it ran. We were about to break this case and I didn't want Michelle to get in harm's way.

"This company is a bogus shell and we have to put an end to it," I said, "but now I'm worried since you've entered the picture."

"Why are you worried about me?"

"What I can tell you is the men who run this company have ties to organized crime. It's best you don't know anything else." These were dangerous people we were dealing with. They were not your everyday petty thieves.

Tara stepped forward and added, "Michelle, Oliver really has been worried about you finding this out. He was never supposed to reveal what he did, not only because it puts you in danger, but it puts the entire team in danger too. It has the potential to expose us and blow our cover."

Michelle's hand covered her neck. I wished Tara hadn't been so blunt, but it was too late now. "I would never tell anyone about this. My lips are sealed."

"What if someone abducts you and holds you hostage? What if you're tortured for information?" Tara asked. "You would easily identify us."

"Jesus, Tara, you're scaring her."

"I know, but she has to understand the gravity of the situation."

Michelle had gone ghostly pale. I reached for her hand

and said, "I think it might be best if you stayed with me from now until we finish our work here."

"And then what?" she asked.

"We'll figure it out later. I don't want you to be alone. You go to work, and come straight home. Either Zack or I will be there. Okay?"

"Does Zack know about this?" Michelle asked.

"Zack is on our team too," I told her.

"Zack too?"

"Yeah. So you'll be safe at my place. Will you do that for me?" I asked.

Tara grabbed her hand, which startled her. "Do it, Michelle. It would make us all feel better knowing you're safe."

She chewed on her lip for a second before she agreed. But then she asked, as an afterthought, "Are you sure you won't mind me being there all the time? And what about Zack?"

"No, it's fine. Zack loves when you're around and you know how I feel about you."

She was so still, I wasn't sure she heard me.

"Michelle, why don't I follow you back to your place where you can pack some clothes?"

She gave a slight nod and stood. She thanked Tara, but was still acting off. I told Tara we would stick to our plan and hopefully this op would be over within the next couple of weeks.

When we got to Michelle's car, I made sure she was okay before I jogged back to mine. An hour later, we pulled into her driveway. Before we went inside, she walked over to my car and reached under the front fender behind the left wheel. Then she handed me the GPS device that had been tracking me.

"Here. You can throw this away, or do whatever you

want with this. I don't need it anymore." Her eyes were cast downward as though she couldn't bear to face me.

"I do have to say it was a bit aggressive."

A bubble of air blew out of her. "Yeah. If you had done this to me I'm not sure I'd be standing where you are."

"There were so many times I wanted to tell you and it killed me to hurt you. I saw it in your eyes every time. I guess that's why I wasn't mad to know you did this." We stood there a bit awkwardly for a moment when I said, "Do you want to go inside?"

"Oh, gosh." She chuckled a little. "My head is swimming with so much stuff, I'm not thinking straight."

"It's fine." I took her elbow and gently led her up the porch steps. Once inside, I had her sit. "So, let me tell you a little bit about myself. Things I couldn't before. I'm from Chicago. That's where I went for Christmas . . . where my parents live. I have a sister, Deanna, who's married to a guy named Randy and a new niece, Ariana, who's almost six months old. I graduated with a degree in computer science, from Carnegie Mellon, and my mom thinks I work at a hospital here in Atlanta in their medical records department.

"Honest to God, Michelle, I think I fell in love with you the night I saw you out on the dance floor. Not a day has passed that I haven't thought about you and wished to fuck I could tell you this story. You are my every fantasy come to life. Sometimes life puts you in the right place at the right time and that happened to me the night I met you. I am not supposed to get involved on a job. But when I met you, you were my shooting star. I couldn't look away for anything and I still can't. Tara gave me a ton of shit about it. But I didn't care. You are my girl, like it or not."

After she stared at me for several long seconds, she said, "Can you please hug me for a minute?"

Was she kidding? I moved to her side and wrapped my arms around her. It was something I'd been dying to do ever since I saw her stuck in that bush in front of that crummy house, all scratched up.

"I've missed you so much, Oliver."

"Not even close to how much I've missed you, Gumdrop. I can't begin to tell you." My hand smoothed her hair and I didn't ever want to let her go.

That nickname got a little laugh out of her. I leaned closer to her and inhaled her scent. The familiar floral fragrance filled my nostrils, sending my dick signals I wasn't quite prepared for. The little fucker needed to be smacked down before he acted like that. But the truth was I wanted her so much. I wanted to feel her silky skin sliding against my own. I wanted to feel her soft pussy sheathed around my dick as I pumped into her. I even wanted her nails to score my skin as she came, panting out my name. Most of all, I wanted her heart, as much as she had mine.

"As much as I'd like to stay here, I think it's best if we get your things and head over to my place."

"Yeah, okay. I should probably text Sheridan to let her know I won't be staying here for a while. We usually talk every day. She might think it's strange if I don't tell her."

"Michelle, you can't tell her any of the details."

"Nothing?"

"Not a word, other than you're staying with me. I'm an undercover agent. Remember?"

She rubbed her forehead. "I'm sorry. I wasn't thinking," she said.

"It's a lot to adjust to."

She disappeared into her room and came back a little while later with a large duffle bag. "I'm ready."

It was fairly late by the time we got to my place. Zack was watching TV when we walked in. Tara must've given him the heads up because he just laughed when we came in. "I've gotta say, I'm fucking happy I don't have to sneak around and say shit behind your back anymore, Michelle." Then he sat up straight and asked her, "What the fuck happened to your face?"

Her fingers flew to her cheek as she lightly touched the scratches there.

"Uh, yeah, I sort of fell into some bushes." She explained what happened and even I didn't know about the paint bucket. It was funny and Zack cracked up. She did too.

"I hate to break this to you, but that's not going to look so good in the morning," I said. "The scratches aren't bad, but it's super puffy and might be even more so when you wake up."

"You think?" she asked.

"Yeah."

"I'm such a klutz."

"You're the prettiest klutz I know," I told her.

"Okay, guys, that's enough. If you're gonna get all gooey and shit, take it upstairs," Zack said.

Michelle parked herself on the couch, much to my dismay, and said, "I have a question for the two of you. Were you all talking business stuff and when I showed up is that why you went silent?"

"Yeah. Every time. I told them to stop because you thought they were talking about you. But they thought they were discreet."

"You guys were giving me a serious complex," she said. "At least I know I'm not crazy. So how many of those people do you work with?"

I hesitated for a second, but Zack jumped in and told

the number in our team. I'm surprised he didn't tell her their real names too. Talk about letting the cat out of the bag. No doubt she would've figured it out anyway. Zack was genuinely fond of Michelle, so he was chatting up a storm with her. I finally caught his eye. All I wanted was a little alone time with her. It had been far too long since we'd been together.

"Well, I'm going to call it a night," he said. "Why don't we plan on a group dinner tomorrow night?"

The fuck. Was he going to want to have a threesome, too?

"Why don't we do that the night after tomorrow. Michelle and I have a lot of catching up to do."

"Oh, sure. It's a plan. Our favorite pizza place—you know the one with the wood-fired grill."

"Yeah. Let's do it. Good night," Michelle said. And we headed up the stairs. I carried her bag for her. It was loaded to the gills, but that was fine by me. She could move in here full time if she wanted.

Once in the room, I helped her get settled. If she wanted space, I would give it to her. But she clung to me like a winter blanket, warm and soft, saying she didn't want to let me go. Finally, she went to wash her face and brush her teeth. When she was finished, I took my turn at the sink, then crawled under the sheets next to her. Her hand immediately went for my dick, which was hard as stone, but tonight wasn't going to be one of those nights. This was about mending what had broken between us. Michelle needed to understand that she wasn't just some woman I had a thing for. Yeah, I told her already, but actions always speak louder, or so they say.

Taking her hand in mine, I brought it to rest over my heart. Then I looked into her beautiful eyes, the ones I dreamed about every night, prayed that I would see again someday, and said, "You have no idea what it means to have you back here with me. Yeah, I've said the words, but I'm not sure you understand the depths of my feelings for you. I wish you could hear my thoughts when I see you, what the sound of your voice does to me, or how your smile affects me. I wish you could feel my heartbeat when I look into your eyes, or know that I fucking get butterflies when you touch me sometimes. My place is here, in your arms, always, if you'll have me. I know this is crazy rushed and you don't have to say anything back, but I wanted you to know that all those times you thought I was with someone else, even if I wasn't in the room with you, I was always there, Michelle. Always."

She grabbed my face and planted her lips on mine. I loved her lips, the way she kissed, all sweet yet fiery at the same time. There were so many things I wanted to say, yet all I wanted to do was hold her tightly and never let her go.

"I love you too, Oliver."

"I'm going to marry you someday. But it has to be when I'm free of this undercover stuff. And the DHS won't be too happy about this. I'm only warning you now."

Her hand rubbed a circle over my heart. "We'll figure it out. Look at Beck and Sheridan. They're making it work. Even after all that stuff they had to deal with. They're going to have a party this summer to celebrate."

"Oh yeah?"

"Yeah. But back to us, we'll make it work. All that matters is Team Oliver and Michelle are back in business."

I kissed her and we soon fell asleep.

Chapter 13

MICHELLE

THE NEXT MORNING, WE WERE ALL DRINKING COFFEE AND eating breakfast while Oliver went into detail with Zack about the GPS tracker I placed on his car. I kind of wanted to slide under the table.

Then Zack held out his hand for a fist bump, which was eye opening. "Dude, you are solid. I can't believe you did that," Zack said.

"Me neither. It's totally creepy. But I was so upset with him."

"No, I think it's cool you thought of it." Zack looked at Oliver then and said, "Would you have thought of that?"

"Yeah, but I doubt I would've done it."

"Hmm. Guess I'm slow then. Did you tell Sheridan?" Zack asked.

"God, no. I didn't tell a soul."

Zack swallowed his coffee. "I'm surprised you didn't say anything since she's your best friend."

"I was ashamed of it."

Then I looked at Oliver, still feeling guilty over it, and asked, "Are you sure you're not mad at me for doing that?"

"No. I deserved it. It's a little stalkerish, but the way I was answering your questions, I was being completely sketchy." Then he looked at Zack and said, "Dude, you're a class act dumbass. You're an undercover government agent who specializes in surveillance and you never would've thought of using a GPS tracker? What the hell is wrong with your brain? Maybe you need to rethink your profession."

"Hey, if you recall, my specialty is computers and hacking, not physically spying on people."

"Yeah, yeah, whatever." Oliver batted his hand through the air.

"Break it up, kids. You two act like you're in elementary school."

"We're like that a lot," Oliver said.

"So how did you end up at the safe house?" Zack asked.

"Safe house?"

That was where I found Oliver, only I wasn't aware it was their safe house. I told him about the times Oliver went there late at night and I worried something happened to one of his parents.

"Oh, shit. So you called and when I never mentioned them, your suspicions totally skyrocketed," Oliver said.

"Yeah. That's why I drove out there. I was sure it involved another woman."

"I get that now."

Zack's head bobbed up and down. Then he said, "You ought to come to work with us."

Oliver's head snapped in Zack's direction so fast I was surprised it didn't spin right off his neck. "Are you fucking crazy? No way do I want my girl involved in something so dangerous."

"We'd keep an eye on her," Zack insisted.

"Just shut up. I can't even go there in my head space." Oliver shuddered. Jeez, what kind of place were they working, and these people they were in with, how terrible were they?

"I'm not sure I even want you back in there," I said.

"We're good. As long as we keep to our jobs, they think we're the usual geeks, following orders, doing our thing. Besides, we only have another week or so there."

"It's going to be a long week," I said.

And it was. My stomach tumbled around like the spin cycle on a washer. It was so twisted in knots I was sure I'd have an ulcer by the end of the week. Even my skin sizzled with anxiety. Every time someone touched me, just the slightest tap would send me jumping out of my seat. One day, a co-worker entered my office and I'd been concentrating so hard on an ad, I didn't hear her. She walked behind me and tapped me on the shoulder. I totally lost it and fell out of my chair. Everyone thought I had gone off the edge. I was legit crazy. And I couldn't explain why . . . couldn't tell them my boyfriend was in real danger at his job. I couldn't even tell my best friend, Sheridan. All this was bottled inside, like a shaken can of soda, ready to explode at any moment.

Late that week Oliver and I had just gotten into bed and were lying there when he heard a noise downstairs.

"Shh, be still."

I froze, wondering who it might be. Zack was in bed already, so I thought maybe he got up for a drink of water or something. "Is it Zack?" I whispered.

Oliver put his finger to his mouth, then reached for his gun on the nightstand. Now that I knew he was an agent, he kept it in the open. Then he got up, indicating that I should stay put. By now, we heard someone coming up the steps.

"Under the bed," he whispered. "Now."

I slipped out of bed and did as he said. I was a freak show, scared to death. Any moment I knew someone was going to barge into the bedroom and kill us. But then I was surprised when I heard a woman's voice call his name. "Oliver, get out here. Now." It was brusque and slightly gravelly sounding.

"Ren? What the hell are you doing here?"

"The op is going down tomorrow and we need to talk. I assume Cupcake is in there with you. We need to get her out of here tonight."

Cupcake? What the hell.

Oliver glanced at me apologetically. "Let's get dressed so we can talk to her."

"Good idea," I snarked. "Does she always waltz into your home unannounced?"

"Pretty much. It's not really my home. The department rented it so it's theirs. I'm sorry."

By this time I was tugging on my pants. "Yeah, well, I'm just glad she didn't crawl into bed with us."

"Actually, so am I."

I flashed him a *you can't be serious* look.

"You'll see when you meet her."

He was right. That woman had a bigger dick than any man alive. Ren—short for Renata—Campini was more ballsy and demanding than anyone I'd ever met. She was sitting in the living room with Zack and some other man by the time we got down there. Introductions were made and his name was Billy Jones. I briefly pondered whether that was his real name before Ren practically yelled at us.

"About fucking time. Did you have to knock off a piece before you joined us? For fuck's sake. Listen up. The entire team's in town. Tomorrow is the big day. We have enough evidence to blow them to Mars, or the fucking moon.

Anyway, I'm taking Cupcake here out to the safe house while Billy debriefs you two." She pointed at Zack and Oliver.

I only stared at this machine of a woman standing there. She wasn't much bigger than me, but damn if she wasn't intimidating. Long mahogany hair, dark eyes, and full red lips made for an attractive package, but I had an image of her pulling out a bullwhip and flaying the hell out of her man. Yeah, I could totally see her as a dominatrix, black leather and all.

"Michelle, are you with us here?" Oliver stared at me.

"Huh?"

"Ren was asking about your work."

"Oh."

"Cupcake, over here." Ren was clicking her fingers at me. "You need to take a day or two off. You can't be alone, so you'll be staying out there with an agent."

"I can call in sick." Ren eyed me like I was a piece of candy. Or maybe prey was a better word. Perhaps she wasn't straight. Who knew? All I knew was she was tough as nails and scared the shit out of me.

Then she clicked her fingers again and said, "Let's go."

My brows drew together as I looked up at Oliver. He jerked his head toward Ren. She wanted me to go with her? Shit.

"I need to pack a bag."

"Then get on it, Cupcake. I don't have all night."

I nudged Oliver and he followed me up the stairs. Once there, I hastily threw some things back into the bag I'd packed a few days ago.

"Oliver, that woman scares me."

He chuckled. "Yeah, Ren is a little freaky. But you'll be in good hands."

"I think she secretly whips her boyfriends."

"Oh, if she did, there would be no secret about it. She's wide open."

"Is she gay?"

"Ren? No. She'll chase after a dick in a heartbeat."

"She doesn't have a thing for you, does she?"

"No," Oliver said, laughing. "She's not into the geeky type. Plus, she doesn't mix business and pleasure."

That should've been a satisfying answer, but it wasn't. I guess I'd just have to paste on a grin and go for it. I kissed Oliver goodbye and he promised to call the next day as soon as everything was over.

Ren and I pulled into the driveway of the safe house about an hour and fifteen minutes later. She talked the whole drive up there, mostly about how wonderful she was. The woman had no lack of self-esteem, at all. When we walked inside, an older man greeted us. His name was Ralph. My internal questions ranged from how they could've come up with a better name than Ralph to how long Ren would be here. I wasn't quite comfortable out here, miles away from anywhere, with two complete strangers. What if these two were serial killers?

Suddenly I blurted, "Would you two mind showing me some ID?"

Ralph's mouth flopped open and Ren cackled like an old woman. Then she said, "Nervous, Cupcake?"

"Um, no," I lied. She could tell.

"Here. Ralph, show her yours. Actually, Cupcake, you should've asked for mine a while back if you had doubts about me."

I didn't until now. And the truth is, I didn't really. But for some reason, I just got slightly freaked. I checked out their IDs and badges and they looked real. I felt better. Then I asked Ralph where I was sleeping because I was tired. He showed me to my room and I crash-landed on the bed. I was asleep in minutes.

My alarm went off, as usual, so I got up and hunted for the bathroom. There appeared to be only one, so I laid claim to it and stole the shower. I didn't linger, just in case someone else needed it. Plus, there was the call I needed to make to my boss. I left my hair to air dry, quickly threw on some clothes, then walked out to the kitchen to find Ralph alone. Ren must've left for the big showdown already.

"Hungry?" Ralph asked.

"Sure, but I'll be happy to make my own breakfast."

He pointed to where everything was so I set off to toast a bagel and pour some coffee. When it was ready, I sat down to eat. Ralph asked about my job so I explained what I did.

"That reminds me, I need to call my boss. It's probably best if I text. I'm an awful liar, so that wouldn't be so good if I flubbed it up."

"You would suck at this job then."

I puffed out a breath. "Yeah, I totally would. When Oliver kept hedging about things, and didn't tell me the truth, it was awful. I could never do that. I would cave. Or I would forget what I told someone and then have to back-track. My mom could always tell when I lied to her."

"You get coached on how to do it during training. The biggest giveaways are not what you say, but the body language."

"I'd fail on all of the above."

Ralph laughed. I took out my phone and texted my boss, telling her I came down with some kind of stomach bug.

"What did you tell your boss?" Ralph asked, and I told him.

He nodded. "So we're stuck here for the time being. I

have some movies, but that's about it. No internet or anything. We can't leave so it's going to be boring, I'm afraid."

Boredom wasn't what killed me. It was worrying about what Oliver was going through. Ralph tried to reassure me, but all of his words did nothing to ease my anxiety. My nerves were exposed wires, sparking at every tiny thing. If there was a lull in our conversation and Ralph suddenly spoke up, I'd jerk.

"Okay, Cupcake, you've got to calm it down."

My hands were trembling. "Why does everyone call me Cupcake?"

"No one is supposed to get involved or take on a love interest while they're in the field. Oliver obviously broke the rule with you. So someone started referring to you as his sweetie pie and then one day someone called you his cupcake and it just stuck."

"Nice, but I hope you know my real name is Michelle."

He threw his head back and laughed. "Got news for you. No one involved with DHS will ever call you that. You'll always be Cupcake to us."

"I guess that's better than Stinkface or Fatbutt."

He laughed even harder.

"Hey, can we take a walk or something?"

"Nope. Sorry. Can't leave the house. Boss' orders."

"Okay. Just checking. I'm super restless."

"What? You don't think I noticed?" He laughed again. I was finding Ralph to be a cheerful sort of man.

"How well do you know Oliver?"

His smile disappeared and he looked mortified. "Oh no. I will not be put in that trap. It happened to me one time before and no way will I fall for that crap again."

"Wait. All I was going to ask you was if you ever worked with him on a case like this."

His posture sagged. "Oh. I thought you were going to drill me with questions about him."

It was my turn to laugh. "I would never do that."

"Good. You women can be sneaky sometimes."

My phone beeped and when I checked it, I saw it was Sheridan.

"Crap. It's my best friend. I can't answer it or she'll know something's up."

"Will she think it weird if you don't?" he asked.

"No. I'll just say I was busy. When do you think we'll hear from them?"

He checked the time and said, "Hopefully soon."

It took a couple more hours before Ralph heard from Ren. Everything went according to their plans. Not much later than that, my phone rang. It was Oliver.

"Are you okay?" I asked.

"Just fine. Busy and tired, but I'm good. Ready to wrap this one up."

"Can I come home?"

"Ren says it's fine so Ralph can drive you in."

A smile the size of Georgia spread clear across my face. "Will you be home tonight?"

"Oh, yeah. Maybe in a couple of hours. Ask Ralph if he minds picking up some pizza for us. It's about the only thing I can think of that's easy."

I did and he gave me a thumbs-up.

"We're good. We'll be waiting."

"Better get enough for Zack, Ren, and Billy too."

"I can manage that. I'll get a variety. Anything to drink?"

"Can you pick up some beer?"

"Yep. I'll handle everything," I said.

"Great. Thanks. Can't wait to see you."

"Same here. I was worried all day."

His voice dropped low, I imagine so no one else could hear. "You shouldn't have, but I'm glad you did. It means you care."

"Care? I love you, you big goob."

He laughed and we ended the call. Ralph and I took off for the city and loaded up on beer and pizza on the way to Oliver's. By the time we got home, the gang was only a few minutes behind us. They all chatted, in a round-about way, about how it all worked out. They wanted to keep me out of the loop, which was fine by me. The less I knew the better.

A few hours later, Ren, Ralph, and Billy left for their hotel. I thanked Ralph for being such a great caretaker.

"No problem, Cupcake. See ya around."

Oliver and I headed upstairs where I found I was so damn exhausted. My eyelids wouldn't stay open for anything. It was Friday night, so it didn't matter. Sleep took over and I gracefully accepted it.

I woke up in the middle of the night to Oliver's tongue in between my thighs. Initially I thought it was a dream, but when he slid a finger inside me, the dream became reality. His lips puckered around my clit, sucking it while his tongue flicked over the tiny bud. Meanwhile, his finger kept up a rhythm that had me coming in no time. Soon his cock, which was long and stiff, was thrusting into my wet pussy. I was ready and willing. He hooked my knee under his arm, lifting my leg up and allowing him to go deeper and harder as he pumped into me. Air rushed out of my lungs with each thrust as he touched me in places that I couldn't remember feeling before. The heated sensations tingled my nerves, setting off pricks of electricity rushing through my veins. Arching my back, I pressed my hips into him, aching to get even closer than I was.

"You're mine now, Gumdrop. All mine," he said as he

pushed into me again and again. And suddenly I was there, falling over the precipice, exploding into another orgasm as I cried out his name. He followed me and we lay in each other's arms, panting and damp with sweat.

"I love you, Michelle."

"Love you too. I need to ask you why you never called me Cupcake."

His body shook. "That's easy. You're not my cupcake. You're my Gumdrop."

Chapter 14

OLIVER

It was a warm summer evening, the day before Sheridan and Beck's party. We'd gone to dinner, and then we went to a park, one of Michelle's favorite places. I had it all planned out. She wasn't aware, of course. There were a lot of things she wasn't aware of, but she would be shortly. This particular park had a beautiful fountain and we sat on the edge, staring at the water display. It was dark now, but the water was lit up, making for an awesome backdrop. My girl looked gorgeous, as always.

It was time. I took her hand and dropped to my knee. She wore a funny expression and it was difficult not to laugh.

"Michelle, you know exactly how I feel about you. I haven't held those emotions back. I love you with everything I have and I promise you, you are far more than anything I could ever have asked for in a partner. I promise to always be there for you, be faithful and encouraging, to inspire you, to lift you up when you're down, laugh with you, cry with you, but most of all, share this journey of life together . . . if you'll have me." Then I asked her to turn around and there were two people behind the fountain holding up a lit sign that said, "Michelle, will you marry me?"

Her hands flew to her face and the tears began to flow.

"I hope those are happy tears?"

She bobbed her head so I pulled out the ring in my pocket. It was a classic round diamond in a tiffany setting. "If you don't like it, we can get whatever you want." I slid it on her finger and her face was as bright as the stars above.

"I love it."

"I guess that's a yes?" I asked.

"Oh, God, yes." Her arms flew around me and I stood, lifting her off her feet. "I have a tiny request. Tomorrow is Beck and Sheridan's party. I think we need to keep this a secret from them until after."

"Agreed. We can make the announcement on Sunday." Then I kissed my bride-to-be.

But she pulled back. "You haven't even met my mom and dad!"

"Yeah I have. I made a little trip down there to ask your dad for your hand."

"You did?" Her eyes bulged out.

"Yep. My mom would've killed me if I hadn't."

She kissed me again, but stopped. "What about your job?"

"They're taking me out of the field and putting me in the local office here. No more undercover stuff."

A huge gush of air burst out of her. "Thank God. I'm not sure my nerves could've handled that."

I pushed her hair back and said, "I know. That last job was stressful on you. I couldn't do that to you all the time. And then when we have kids, I would hate to leave."

"Kids?" she asked.

"You do want them, don't you?"

"Uh, maybe."

"You will. Trust me."

"How can you be so sure? You haven't met my cousins. They may change your mind."

I kissed her to take her mind off it. We were going to have kids. I wanted a tiny Michelle to hold in my arms. When I thought back to Ariana, it made me remember how soft she was.

"What are you thinking?"

"That I can't wait for you to meet my family. They're gonna love you."

"When?" she asked.

"When are you gonna meet them?"

"No, when are we gonna get married?"

I cupped her face in my hands and said, "It's up to you. I'm just glad you said yes. I'm also glad I saw you that night. You were mine from the beginning and now you'll be my Gumdrop forever."

The End

Acknowledgements

THANK YOU TO ALL THE READERS WHO CONTINUE TO support me in this crazy world. You have so many books to choose from but the fact you chose mine rocks my world. Without you, I wouldn't be living my dream.

Thank you to Angel Justice, the dream child of this project and for inviting me to join this group. When she came to me and told me about it, I was super excited to a part of The Vault. How exciting to bring a group of talented authors together in such a way, and then again when we release our second novellas later this year. I hope you readers are just as excited as we are.

I wouldn't ever publish a book without the help of my closest friend and sometimes co-author, Terri E. Laine, so another huge thanks goes out to her. I don't know what I'd do without her. She's the vanilla to my chocolate.

My beta readers deserve the biggest shout out too: Andrea, Kristie, Heather, Kat, and Ashley. You guys are amazing and I would be lost without your help.

And I can't leave without giving a shout out to my Hellions in Hargrove's Hangout. Keep raising it y'all!

Stalk A.M. Hargrove

If you would like to hear more about what's going on in my world, please subscribe to my mailing list on my website at amhargrove.com.
You can also join my private group—Hargrove's Hangout — on Facebook if you're up to some crazy shenanigans! Please stalk me. I'll love you forever if you do. Seriously.

www.amhargrove.com
Twitter @amhargrove1
www.facebook.com/amhargroveauthor
www.facebook.com/anne.m.hargrove
www.goodreads.com/amhargrove1
Instagram: amhargroveauthor
Pinterest: amhargrove1
annie@amhargrove.com

For Other Books by A.M. Hargrove visit
www.amhargrove.com

For The Love of English
For The Love of My Sexy Geek (The Vault Anthology)
I'll Be Waiting (The Vault Anthology — April 2018)
A Special Obsession
Chasing Vivi
Craving Midnight
From Ashes To Flames (April 2018)

Cruel and Beautiful
A Mess of a Man
One Wrong Choice
A Beautiful Sin
Worth Every Risk (March 2018)

The Wilde Players Dirty Romance Series:
Sidelined
Fastball
Hooked

The Edge Series:
Edge of Disaster
Shattered Edge
Kissing Fire

The Tragic Duet:
Tragically Flawed, Tragic 1
Tragic Desires, Tragic 2

The Hart Brothers Series:
Freeing Her, Book 1
Freeing Him, Book 2
Kestrel, Book 3
The Fall and Rise of Kade Hart

Sabin, A Seven Novel
The Guardians of Vesturon Series

A.M. Hargrove

ONE DAY, ON HER WAY HOME FROM WORK AS A SALES manager, USA Today bestselling author, A. M. Hargrove, realized her life was on fast forward and if she didn't do something soon, it would be too late to write that work of fiction she had been dreaming of her whole life. So she made a quick decision to quit her job and reinvented herself as a Naughty and Nice Romance Author.

Annie fancies herself all of the following: Reader, Writer, Dark Chocolate Lover, Ice Cream Worshipper, Coffee Drinker (swears the coffee, chocolate, and ice cream should be added as part of the USDA food groups), Lover of Grey Goose (and an extra dirty martini), #WalterTheP-uppy Lover, and if you're ever around her for more than five minutes, you'll find out she's a non-stop talker. Other than loving writing about romance, she loves hanging out with her family and binge watching TV with her husband. You can find out more about her books www.amhar-grove.com.

Bonus Material from For The Love of English

Prologue—Beck

About Six Years Ago

"BECK, you'd better get in here."

It's still dark, but then again, it is December and the sun won't rise until seven thirty. But I'm home for Christmas break, so why is my dad waking me up so damn early?

"What?" I groan.

"Just get your butt out of bed and get in here. Now."

When he uses that tone, I know not to argue. So I drag my ass out of my warm and toasty bed and shuffle into the kitchen. My parents stand by the island, looking into a large cardboard box as my mother stuffs a letter into my hands.

"What's this?" I ask.

"I don't know, but it was on top of this." She points at the box.

"A Christmas gift?" he asks. "A little early."

"I wouldn't say it's early if I were you," my dad answers.

Rubbing the sleep out of my eyes, I attempt to clear my head. I'd partied hard last night. All the guys got together as they usually did when everyone came in town from college. I barely remember what time I came home last night.

"Can someone tell me what this is all about?"

All of a sudden, a baby starts crying.

My mother says, "Well, we were hoping you could shed a little light on this."

"Whose baby is that?" I ask.

"Beck, read the damn letter!" My father's patience comes to an end. "It was in the box with the baby on the front porch. I walked outside to get the paper, and there it sat. Now, read the letter so we can get some answers."

I look at the envelope in his hand. Sure enough, my name is scrawled across it. I tear open the seal and pull out a folded page of paper, the kind with the lines you tear off from a spiral notebook. I rub my fingers across those little tags left behind because suddenly I'm scared, totally freaked out. I don't want to read what's on this piece of paper.

Raising my eyes, I instantly feel five years old again when the accusatory gazes of my parents drill holes into me. I swallow, but my saliva has taken a hike to places unknown.

In a soft voice, Mom urges, "Beck."

Nodding, I unfold the paper and read.

BECK,

I tried. I really did. But it was too much. So I'm giving her to you. She was a lot more than I bargained for. If you don't want her, then you can give her up for adoption. In the box under her blankets, you'll find the legal papers, signed by a lawyer and me, which give total custody to you. I've given up all legal rights to her. If you're wondering, she was conceived homecoming night at the fraternity party in November our freshman year. I doubt you even remember since we were both drunk. I don't blame you, as the fault was mine as much as yours. On the documents, you'll find my name. I'm sure you will follow up with DNA testing, which I encourage you to do. But you are her father, as you were the only one I was with. In the envelope with her legal documents, I've also enclosed her medical records. She is healthy—if you're wondering. That's not why I'm leaving her with you. And so you know, I couldn't go through with the abortion I scheduled.

I'm sorry. I guess I wasn't cut out for motherhood.
Abby

I'M COMPLETELY STUNNED, frozen.

"Well?" Dad asks. I hand over the letter. And then I somehow summon up the courage to peek into the box and get my first glimpse of my daughter—the daughter whose name I don't even know. The deepest blue-green eyes lock onto my own, and I can't breathe for what seems like an eternity. Because I'm staring into a mirror. All I want to do is touch her, but I'm scared to death. I've never held a baby before. Will I hurt her? Is she fragile?

"Go on. Pick her up, Beck," Mom says.

My shaking arms reach for her, and her pink blankets fall away to unveil a tiny body encased in a pale pink one-piece suit as her arms and legs flail about. Her small head is layered in pale fuzz, and I rub my cheek against it. It's the softest stuff I've ever felt, and I don't want to let her go.

"Well, kiddo, looks like you got yourself a kid," my father grumbles.

Mom chuckles and says, "Looks like you've got yourself a granddaughter."

"Dad, did you read the letter?" I ask.

"Yep."

"Will you check her medical records? I want to know her name."

Dad ruffles some papers around, and he finally says, "Hmm. Says here it's English. English Beckley Bridges."

"English." What the hell am I gonna do with a baby?

Suddenly, a loud sounding prrrft escapes as I feel the vibrations on my hand. The room fills with a noxious odor.

"Ugh, what's that?" I ask.

Dad laughs, roots around in the box, and hands me a plastic pad. "I know one thing you're gonna be doing. Looks like you're gonna be changing a diaper. Make that plural." I hear him laughing all the way down the hall.

ONE
PRESENT DAY

MY SCRUTINIZING GLANCE takes in all the trimmings and accessories I've strategically placed on every wall, looking for any little fault I can find. There isn't much left of my nails as I chew them down to the quick while I analyze my decorating skills. I frown, admitting to myself it's apparent why I chose the profession I did. No doubt my roommate would waltz in here and have a dozen or more ideas on how to make this room much more appealing to the eye. She'd probably recommend hand-sewn decorative pillows strewn about with lavish artwork hung on the walls and those cool things you see on Pinterest made out of used pallets. And most likely, she'd have all new desks made out of them with little cubbyholes for pencils and slots for books. Unfortunately, my budget and time won't allow for that. My stomach quivers in anticipation, but why shouldn't it? It's the first day of school. My *very first* day. This is the moment I've been waiting for and working toward my whole life. Okay, maybe not my *whole* life, but whatever. In a few minutes, twenty-two six-year-old kids will be running through the door, minds like sponges, and if I'm not prepared to be the very best sponge filler in the world to them, I will forever destroy their love and zest for learning.

Melodramatic much? Maybe. I am a first grade teacher, and it's my overwhelming duty to offer them a chance to love school. If I fail, they will hate school forever, and it will all be on my shoulders. And to top it all off, this is my very first day as a bona fide teacher. I just graduated from college, so this is it. My chance to change the world! My dream job, my career, and my path I've chosen.

Clearing out the toxic carbon dioxide, I fill my eager lungs with a dump truck load of fresh oxygen. And then I hear them. The pounding of minuscule feet on tiled floors and the screaming of young voices. In the midst of all that, I can hear Susan Jorgensen, the principal, telling the children to calm down and line up, single file in the hall. I stifle a giggle because I can remember hearing those very same words from my own principal. The door swings open, and Susan sticks her head inside.

"Miss Monroe, are you ready to meet your new students?"

"I am." I cross my fingers and pray.

She holds the door open, and a line of kids, resembling marching ants, walks into the room. A smile replaces my frown, and I can't help but feel the excitement replace my anxiety. They look scared to death, but if cute could be a picture, it would be lined up in front of me. Oh. My. God. How can I not fall in love with every single one of these mites? I am going to be mashed potatoes with them.

"Good morning, everyone. My name is Miss Monroe, and I'm going to be your teacher this year. How is everyone today?"

One little boy immediately pops a thumb into his mouth, and his bottom jaw goes to town. A few of the girls offer me a shy grin, and a couple of the boys look around and don't give me the time of day. Susan catches my eye, points to the door, and heads out. I have prearranged seating, so I go to the front row and start calling out names and seating the children. When I'm about halfway down the second row, I get to the name, English Bridges, and no one responds, so I keep on. I have about three-quarters of the students seated when the door bursts open, and a woman, who is perhaps in her late forties, stands with a child clinging to her neck.

"I'm so sorry to interrupt, but is this the first grade classroom?" she asks out of breath.

"Yes, it is," I answer, smiling. "Can I help you?"

"I'm sorry we're late. I'm Anna Bridges, and this is English. English Bridges."

"Oh, yes."

"Would you mind if I had a word in the hall with you?"

I glance at the unseated students and say, "Can you

give me a couple of minutes to seat the rest of the students?"

"Sure." I watch her exit and then finish with the rest of the children.

"Now, all of you remain in your seats, and I'll be right back. Remember, no getting out of your seats. Do you understand me?"

"Yes," they all answer. I walk into the hallway, and Anna Bridges stands there, still holding English.

"Is English all right?" I ask.

Anna rolls her eyes at me. Of course, English can't see her. I wonder what this is all about.

"She's fine. She just has a case of I-don't-want-to-go-to-school, but I told her that if she didn't come, she would grow up to be intellectually challenged."

I hear a muffled voice say, "I will not be intellectually challenged. I'm smart. You said so. I can learn on those school videos I see on TV."

Hmm. This one's quite precocious, so I ask, "But, English, wouldn't you miss out on making friends and having all sorts of fun at school?"

"School's not fun."

"Hmm. Didn't you like kindergarten?"

"Yes," she mumbles.

"Then how do you know you won't like first grade if you've never been?"

Her shoulders practically meet her ears as she gives me an exaggerated shrug.

"Tell you what. Why don't you try it for a week? Then you can decide if you like it or not."

The little girl lifts her head and turns to look at me. A head full of blond ringlets greets me highlighted by a pair of blue-green eyes. But what also captures my attention is she's dressed in a kaleidoscope of colors—striped leggings and a flowery shirt that somehow go together on her. This one will have me wrapped around her pinky in no time flat. I'm not sure who will be teaching whom.

"Okay. But you promise I'll like it?"

"I can't make that kind of promise, English, but I'll do my best."

She turns back around to face the woman and says, "Come on. Let's go."

"Oh, sweetie, I'm leaving you here."

"Noo! You can't leave me, Banana!"

Banana?

The woman looks at me and grins. "Yup, she calls me her Banana. Great substitute for Grandma Anna, huh?"

The confusion must be flashing on my face like neon.

The woman clarifies it. "Since my name is Anna, I had this brainiac idea that instead of just Grandma, I'd have her call me Grandma Anna, but she couldn't get that mouthful out, so it turned into her Banana. It's gotten better. I used to be her Big Banana. Nice, huh? I'm the brunt of many jokes."

I cover my mouth to stop the rush of laugher that threatens.

"So, you're the grandmother, then?"

"Yes, my son is out of town, so I have parenting duties until tomorrow. Oh, I nearly forgot. Can you accept texts during school hours? He's so nervous about not being here for her first day, so I told him I'd run interference, but he'd love a text or two from you, if at all possible today."

It makes my heart happy to see a parent so involved. After all the horror stories I've heard during my student teaching about how parents don't care anymore, I'm thrilled about this.

"We encourage parents to email, but in this case, I'll be

happy to text him. I can't imagine how worried he is. Can you leave me his number?"

She quickly hands me a note with a name and number on it. "I'll let him know you'll text and tell him your name."

"Perfect. Are you ready, English, to start your education?"

She gives me her little hand, and before we head inside the room, she yells out, "Banana, tell Daddy I'm under the rainbow today."

"Okay, Munchkin, I will." She gives English a smile and a thumbs-up. I guess "under the rainbow" is a good thing, then.

When we walk inside, all things good turn topsy-turvy and the classroom is mayhem. Students are running wild, chasing each other, and yelling like they are on the playground. I need to take control. I waste no time in walking to the front of the class and clapping my hands. It does no good. Then I say, "Students, take your seats." No response. You'd think it was a free-for-all. I stick my fingers in my mouth and let the biggest, loudest whistle loose. If there's one thing I can do, it's whistle.

They all come to a freezing halt and turn to me.

"Did I not ask you to remain in your seats?"

They nod.

"When I ask you a question, I expect you to respond with words, not gestures. That means you either say, 'Yes, Miss Monroe or no, Miss Monroe.' Is that clear?"

"Yes, Miss Monroe."

"So, did I not give clear instructions that you were to remain in your seats?"

"Yes, Miss Monroe."

I sweep my arm in front of me, asking, "Is this remaining in your seats?"

"No, Miss Monroe."

"And that's really quite a shame because I had a special treat for all of you today, but since we've only been in class for fifteen minutes, and you can't seem to follow my instructions in this short period of time, it looks like there will be no treats for anyone today."

"Oh, Miss Monroe, we're sorry. We didn't think you'd care," a little girl pipes up.

"All of you take your seats, please." I wait for them to be seated and show English to her desk. Once everyone is sitting, I say, "I do care. If I didn't, I wouldn't have said to stay seated in the first place. And ... if you have any doubt or question my instructions, all you have to do is check with me."

English raises her hand.

"Yes, English."

With a big grin, she asks, "Since I wasn't bad, can I get a treat?"

I can already tell this child is quite clever.

"We'll see. But first, what I'd like to do is go around the room and have everyone say their names so we can all get to know each other."

Sometime during the hectic morning, I remember to send a text to Beckley Bridges.

Your mother asked me to let you know how English's first day is going, and I'm happy to report she's doing very well. Feel free to text me back at any time. Sheridan Monroe

I anticipate a quick response since Anna indicated how nervous he was about his daughter's first day of school, but I hear nothing. Maybe he was busy and didn't see it, so I let it go. I check my phone an hour later, when I'm able to break away from my team of tiny monsters, and still no answer. It makes me wonder if he ever got the text, so I send him another.

Hi, Mr. Bridges, it's Sheridan Monroe, English's teacher. Just checking in to let you know the day is going well for her. She hasn't missed a beat and is already making friends.

There isn't time for me to wait for a reply. The students are raising Cain about something, and when I check, English is in the middle of the altercation. She's telling all the boys she can "take them down because she's a tomboy."

"Okay, we'll have none of that in here. That's not nice talk, English."

English stomps her foot and says, "He pushed me, Miss Monroe, and I told him not to do that anymore, but he did it again. My daddy told me not to allow anyone to bully me."

And how do you argue with that?

"Jordan, did you push English?"

"No."

Someone is lying, and I need to find out.

"Okay, one of you isn't telling the truth. Who in this room saw what happened?"

Melanie, a dark-haired shy girl, steps forward. "They both are."

So now I have the equivalent of a soap opera taking place.

"Melanie, can you tell me what happened?"

She bobs her head up and down. "He pushed her, and she said to stop. And then she said she could take all the boys in here down."

I look at English, and her lower lip sticks out. She wears the badge of guilt quite well.

"So let this be a lesson. There will be no bullying in this classroom, or on the playground by either boys or girls. Does each of you understand me?"

A chorus of "Yes, Miss Monroe," comes back to me.

"Good. So this time, no punishment will take place, but if this happens again, I'll be forced to report it to the principal." A sea of solemn faces greets me.

The rest of the day passes without event, and at the end of the day, I walk my students to the exit. When I return to my desk, I check my phone and notice I never received a response from Mr. Bridges. So much for the caring father I had him pegged for.

And that's how my first day of school goes.

TWO

"SO, HOW WAS YOUR FIRST DAY?" my roommate, Michelle, asks.

"Ugh. They are fierce. You don't ever get a break. I mean, I can't leave the room to pee. And I mean it."

"Oh, come on."

"No, I'm serious. And I have this one little girl, English, who is a … I'm not quite sure how to describe her. She told the boys she could take every one of them down."

Michelle spits out her wine. "No shit!"

"Yes, shit. And what do you say to that? Booyah? I wanted to die laughing, but I couldn't."

"That's epic."

I rub my eyes because my contacts are stinging like fire. "I hope I don't let these kids down." The memory of what my teachers did for me, and the quest for constant discovery of new ideas they instilled in me makes me want to be the very best at what I do. Suddenly, I have giant doubts over my abilities.

"What's that look for?" Michelle knows me too well.

"Nothing."

She points a finger at me. "Nothing my rear end. I know you better than you know yourself."

"It's just I never want to let my students down."

"You won't. And do you know why?"

"Why?"

"Because you are the most caring person I know. That's why. Now stop worrying."

It's easy to care about others when you don't have anyone who cares about you. Well, almost anyone. Michelle cares. A boatload. Unless she has a new boyfriend, and then she gets boy obsessed.

"Now what are you thinking about?"

I look her square in the eye and speak the truth. "How nice it would be to tell my mom and dad about my first day as a teacher."

"Yeah, and they would be so proud of you, Sheridan. You have to know that, right?"

She's right. I do know that. But the fact remains that they're gone, and they're no longer here to talk to or to tell things to anymore. Or to bounce ideas off of or to ask them for advice. Or to run home to when I just plain and simple need a hug. It's not easy being alone. Not that I want to complain, because honestly, it doesn't do any good, and it sure as hell won't bring either of them back.

"Don't be sad, Sher. This is what you've worked so hard for. And you're going to be the teacher that every kid remembers and every parent praises."

"Promise?"

"Promise."

The next morning, my little army of ants marches in. Once they're seated, I ask for their homework from the day before. For the most part, with the exception of a few minor squabbles, the day is going remarkably well. I even hand out my treats from the previous day, since everyone is behaving so admirably. Our mid-morning snack time arrives and time for the brief rest period. Soon it's lunchtime, and I breathe a sigh, desperate for a break. The cafeteria monitors take over, and since I'm not a monitor this week, I head to the teachers' lounge to eat.

"How's it going, Sheridan?" I look over my shoulder to see Susan, the principal, behind me.

"Whew, those little buggers can wear you out, can't they?"

She laughs and says, "You bet. They are relentless. Any problems so far?"

"None. They seem to be a bright bunch."

"Yeah, their test scores indicated that. I think you'll have a challenging year, though, because of it."

"As long as they love to learn, I'm good with that."

"Sheridan, the trick is getting that love to stick with them."

"I know. And that's my goal. Make learning fun and interesting."

The room fills as other teachers trickle in, and someone pulls Susan away. She's been wonderful so far, and I hope she continues to be the kind of principal who will support my classroom decisions. Right now, I get great vibes from her. Let's hope it continues that way.

I finish up my lunch and make my way back to the classroom. On my way there, I stick my head inside the cafeteria to see how my students are acting. I see the usual of hands grabbing each other's food, but everything seems fine.

After lunch, we sail through our math and science exercises, and toward the end of the day, I decide to play a game.

"How about we have some fun? Who wants to play a game?"

They all get excited and jump out of their seats. In the corner of the room, I have a chair I use for story time, so I have them move there and I bring the big alphabet chart.

"Let's all say the ABC's." And they do. When they finish, we start the game. "Okay, who can name something that starts with an A?"

Everything is great until we get to the letter V. That seems to be giving them trouble until English raises her hand and yells out, "I know, I know. Vagina!"

Twenty-one sets of curious eyes laser in on her, and when she doodles around like everything is perfectly normal, they focus on me. But before I can speak, English blurts out, "You know," and her thumb jabs down in the direction of said vagina. It's like twenty-one heads watching a tennis match. They look at her, then me. I've become mute; all capability to speak has been stripped away. I was told to expect the unexpected, but this takes it to a completely new level.

And then … English adds the cake topper. "You know, it's where the penis goes."

For the love of everything, why me? It quickly rolls downhill from there. Robert shoves his hands into his pockets and stares right at English's crotch. I know exactly what he's thinking, and I know I need a quick change of topic, but as soon as I open my mouth, Millicent shouts out, "My little brother has a penis. He had an operation on it when he was born, and my mom had to clean it every day." And then she giggles. "When he pee-pees, it shoots up in the air if Mommy forgets to put a diaper on it."

English adds, "I don't have a baby brother. Only my daddy. I'm sure his penis is big, though, because my daddy is big."

"Okay, everyone, who can think of something that starts with the letter W?"

"Miss Monroe, why is your face so red?"

Because we're talking about penises and vaginas, for the love of God. "Hmm, I guess it's a bit warm in here. So, who wants to take a try at the letter W?"

I could barely pay attention due to the debacle that occurred. I pray none of the kids go home and recount what happened. Oh my God. What if they do? Susan will kill me. I vaguely hear one of them say the word *whale*.

"Miss Monroe? Do whales have penises?" Now even the boys want to know.

"Okay, great. Whale is a good word. Now what about X? That's a tough one," I say enthusiastically.

"X-rated," English screams, jumps up and down, and claps her hands. What kind of house does this child live in? I don't even know what to say to this.

"That's not quite a word, English. Can we choose another?"

Miguel hollers, "X-ray!"

Whew. "Very good, Miguel."

I can see I've hurt English's feelings, but I'm not sure what to do. Maybe she'll get the final letter. "And anyone for the letter Z?"

About five students yell, "Zebra!" Most of the kids are laughing, but not English. Her blond curls dangle as her chin touches her chest.

"Very good, class, and just for being such excellent participants, I have a surprise for all of you." I hand out some homemade chocolate chip cookies to each student.

When I get to English, she mutters, "No, thank you."

"Why don't you take it home then, and maybe you can have it later?" It sits on her desk, and she looks terribly forlorn. My tone must've been harsher than I thought. I'll have to take care with her. She must be really sensitive.

The bell rings, signaling the end of class, and the kids all line up to make the march down the hall. Susan runs a tight ship, which is a good thing. I watch the students as they run to their respective cars or buses, but English seems so sad. I can't stop thinking about her. And it lasts all night.

Made in the USA
Columbia, SC
22 March 2018